Also by Fuminori Nakamura

The Thief
Evil and the Mask
Last Winter, We Parted
The Gun
The Kingdom
The Boy in the Earth
Cult X

MY
ANNIHILATION

FUMINORI NAKAMURA

Translated from the Japanese by SAM BETT

Watashi No Shometsu by Fuminori Nakamura
Copyright © 2016 by Fuminori Nakamura
Translation copyright © 2022 by Sam Bett

Original Japanese edition published by Bungeishunju Ltd., in 2016.
English translation rights reserved by Soho Press Inc., under the
license granted by Fuminori Nakamura arranged with Bungeishunju
Ltd., through The English Agency (Japan) Ltd.

First published in English by Soho Press, Inc.
Soho Press
227 W 17th Street
New York, NY 10011

Library of Congress Cataloging-in-Publication Data
Names: Nakamura, Fuminori - author. | Bett, Sam - translator.
Title: My annihilation / Fuminori Nakamura ; translated from the
Japanese by Sam Bett. | Other titles: Watashi no shometsu English
Description: New York : Soho Crime, [2022]
Identifiers: LCCN 2021029617

ISBN 978-1-64129-272-6
eISBN 978-1-64129-273-3
International Paperback ISBN 978-1-64129-363-1

Subjects: LCGFT: Novels. | Thrillers (Fiction)
Classification: LCC PL873.5.A339 W3713 2022
DDC 895.63/6—dc23
LC record available at https://lccn.loc.gov/2021029617

Printed in Canada

10 9 8 7 6 5 4 3 2 1

Turn this page, and you may give up your entire life.

A cramped room in a rundown mountain lodge, and on the desk a manuscript, left open to page one, as if it had been waiting here for ages to be read.

The only other piece of furniture a simple bed. The wood floor creaked with every step. The slight breeze was enough to set the thin glass of the tired window rattling.

My thoughts went to the various forms of identification in my bag. An insurance card, a certificate of residence, even a pension booklet, all under the name Ryodai Kozuka. Born in 1977, he was two years older than me. Japanese standards for applying for IDs are a joke. None of these cards had a photograph of me, but I could use them to apply for a passport that did. Trading places with Ryodai Kozuka.

I looked at the text of the pages. The paper was old, bound simply with a clip. This manuscript had to have been written by Ryodai Kozuka. An account, or even the life story, of the man whose place I was about to take.

A white suitcase stood in the corner of the room. My heart beat a little faster. I hadn't brought that suitcase here. That must be where it was. Kozuka's body. Trees danced outside the window, as if to tell me of the sinister nature of this place. But I had understood immediately what to do. Bury that suitcase in the forest, and this would all be over.

"Turn this page, and you may give up your entire life." Or so the first page said. But I had no intention of giving my old life up. He might have left behind unfinished business, but it was no business of mine. All I wanted was his identity.

The light from the scrawny desk lamp cast an orange glow over the dust. I lit a cigarette and turned the page of the shoddy manuscript.

I guess it started with the funeral.

A girl who lived nearby was kidnapped and discovered dead. The younger sister of one of my classmates. People sweating through their black funeral clothes milled awkwardly about. I was in the third grade, and watched these strangers dressed in black surround my classmate. His parents stood nearby, holding a portrait of the lost girl.

They had apprehended an unemployed man in his thirties, who went on to testify to having lured the girl into his car and murdered her when she began to kick and scream. The man had a hulky build and wore ratty basketball shoes. I had seen him wandering around town several times, leaning a little forward as he walked.

My classmate had told me that he never liked

his sister, who happened to have a different father. I suppose he told me because I also had a sister I disliked who had a different father.

When the hall had started to clear out, I went over to say something to him. My mouth dried up. My breath was shallow. The murder of the girl and the man they had arrested were plenty scary as it was, but what really terrified me was my classmate. I addressed him in a whisper. The range of lights decking the funeral hall transformed the tense figures of the strangers into shafts of shadow on the floor. The shadows overlapped, forming peculiar geometric shapes on the linoleum.

". . . What happened?"

I had a feeling this was all because of him. That he had flaunted his pretty little sister in front of the giant man. A man without a job, left to nurse his dark side—or perhaps the dark side had expanded on its own—as he wandered miserably around town. Had my classmate dangled his sister at the man the way that you might tease a stray dog with a piece of meat?

Back then I didn't know the term existed, but I suspected this was what they call a perfect crime. Without dirtying his own hands, he had provoked this crazed, dangerous prowler to attack her. But now my classmate looked at me as if he didn't understand, eyes bleary with tears. I realized my assumption had been wrong. My classmate's parents patted his head, trying to reassure him. The line of strangers did the same. An ugly feeling welled up inside of me. It was a gross warmth, pulsing through my neck and cheeks. I stared at him in a daze, like I was jealous. Surrounded by the overlapping shafts of shadow.

This goes without saying, but my current self is putting words into my own mouth at a younger age. Back then, my mind was hazy. I was ashamed of my fantasies, but they refused to go away, as if possessed of their own will.

That evening, I went back to my so-called home. When my sister saw me, she started crying and ran to Grandma—my stepfather's mother, so we weren't connected by blood. My sister said that I had hit her, claimed that I had lied about the funeral, that I'd been picking on her the entire time.

Grandma calmed my sister down, saying, "Let Grammy take care of this." Then it was the two of us. This time, though, she realized that my sister was lying. She had a long ruler, the color of clay. A stiff ruler that looked accustomed to its secondary function. I knew how to handle what was about to happen. She was barely going to tap me. All I had to do was scream like I was on fire, and Grandma would let up, skittish as she was. That ruler didn't scare me nearly as much as the story of the murder, the giant man they had arrested, the murder of the little girl. Grandma set it down on the tatami and stared at me. Her left eye was cloudy and yellow. That eyelid sometimes twitched, a symptom of weak nerves.

Grandma's son was my sister's father, but my mom gave birth to me before she ever met him.

"I know you didn't do it, but you've given her a scare. You understand?"

How could I possibly understand? I'd never hit my sister once.

Grandma wouldn't back down. She loved my sister more than life itself. Her affection for my sister filled her nearly to the brim, so that her days were plagued by the conviction that a threat was always close at hand, a fear which manifested as a dizzying pain that tortured her. What started as love had devolved into a hysteria that she took out on others.

Both of us knew my sister was on the other side of the door, waiting for me to take a whooping. I stared back at Grandma with a face that said that she could hit me if she wanted. I could take it. It would be okay. Just get it over with. When I looked at someone like this, with a sparkle in my eye, I always felt a warmth well up inside of me that was borderline enjoyable. She swung the ruler, slapping the tatami floor in front of me. We heard my sister scurry off. This only reinforced my understanding of how adults behaved.

Grandma stood up, looking distraught, and

frowned at me, the eyelid of her murky left eye twitching. Like she was asking me what I was doing in her house. Like I was ruining the world for her. To her, I was an intruder, standing in the way of what could have been a happy home. My existence is what made her eyelid twitch.

Later that night, I left the room that had been chosen for me, hoping to sleep with my mom for the first time in years. I must have been horrified by what was happening in town, and scared enough of my own thoughts I needed comfort from her. Or maybe the murder had brought something up, a feeling that I wanted her to calm. The hallway was cold against my bare feet, as if refusing to warm up to me. If I told my mom my stomach hurt, I figured she would come back to my room.

I stopped in front of the door because I heard a voice. It was Dad talking to Mom.

"She cried again today though, right? What the hell? Why can't they act like siblings and get along?"

"I'm sorry. I tell them the same thing all the time."

"Look, this has become a problem. I've even got Ma pestering me about it. Come home from fighting at the office to a fight in my own house."

"I'm sorry."

"You do realize when you look at me like that, it's like you're blaming this on me. Is that what you think?"

"I'm . . ."

I heard Dad hit Mom. My heart sped up. This always happened. Every time I heard that sound, my legs went weak and all my muscles stiffened up.

". . . I'm not the kind of dad who beats his kids. Those guys are scum. But you, you're all grown up. So tell me, why can't they get along? Don't you hate it when they fight? Why is everybody always fighting?"

The sounds of Dad hitting Mom continued. Mom let out little shrieks. It was all that I could do to stand in front of the door. The silver doorknob glimmered idly through the darkness. The door was incredibly rickety and thin. Open it, and my entire life could transform in an instant.

Dad's violence escalated. Mom's stifled shrieks grew louder. But then something peculiar happened. Soon my father's breath went ragged, the floor boomed like they were sumo wrestling, and my mother's shrieks became something more like breathing, like she was struggling but enjoying it. The pounding of the floor continued. Were they doing it again? I'd seen it happening just once, for half a second. Dad smothering Mom like he was stealing her from me forever, but Mom making noises like she was enjoying it. The door whispered to me. *Open it and see—Why not take a long, hard look this time? See something that'll really shake your little mind at the root.* For whatever reason, the voice sounded a lot like this character on an anime I watched.

If you watch them long enough, you may never be the same again.

But I went back to my room and headed straight for my stuffed animal. I was embarrassed for being so girly, but I told myself that having a stuffed animal was fine, as long as the animal was something manly.

It seemed like Mom and Dad were as upset as me about all the stuff happening around town.

There were probably more of them out there. Other crazy people, besides the guy they had arrested. I pictured crazy people smothering us all, the entire crowd of stupid strangers that were up in arms because someone had died. The crazy giants pressed us down and wrung our necks like it was nothing. We had a new reason to be terrified.

I had a place where I could go. A place I went when it was hard to breathe.

The house was built on high land. Old train tracks went right past the back door. Hop over the guardrail and climb up into the woods, and you reached a clearing on the hillside, where you could look out over the entire town. The space was about twelve feet across. It dropped off in a sheer cliff, but the view was wide open and free.

I used to spend a lot of time sitting up there. What I remember most is looking at the trees.

I must have thought those trees were pretty lucky. Nothing to think about or do but keep on standing. When I was up there, in the midst of the tall trees, I could let go of my loneliness and feel part of a whole. Hard to say if I was ascribing human qualities to the trees or denying those same qualities from myself. But when night came, it felt like the trees were closing in on me and glaring down, objects of terror.

Even scarier was how they swayed in the wind. But sometimes I would stay there, sticking it out. Thinking this would make me stronger. As if being able to stay put meant that I could take whatever else would come along. So I stayed put, in the darkness, swallowed by the expressionless swaying trees. I tested myself like this all the time, eager to step up when me and my classmates dared each other to do things. It wasn't some death wish; it was a ritual to make me stronger.

Why would I bring my sister to a special place like this? She had been bugging me about it for a while. Once she was aware that I was sneaking off somewhere, she begged me to take her along. My sister wasn't always hostile toward me. True, her childish evil streak took over when she felt insecure, but most of the time she was a cute, smiley kid. She must have recognized intuitively that I was an intruder and felt confused by the imbalance that I represented. When she heard about the funeral, I guess she childishly assumed that it was me who died. She was overwhelmed enough with sadness and relief that seeing me come home pushed her over the edge.

To apologize for hitting her, I brought my sister to the place. Hitting her is something I had never done, of course, but my childish sister saw it as a fact; and while I knew, however childish myself, that it was not a fact, I still felt guilty.

When we arrived, my sister cried out with delight. It was late already, so we took a quick look and went home. That night in bed, though, I was unable to calm down, haunted by a vision of my sister tumbling off the cliff.

The next day, I told her that she wasn't going back there. It was not okay for her to go up there alone. This made her sulk. She said that just because I was her older brother (her choice of words) didn't mean I owned the place. It was hers too.

An anxious feeling grew inside of me. Every day, when my sister came home, I felt relieved to see her. When I asked her, "Did you go up to the place?" she sometimes nodded.

"You're not supposed to go there."

"It's fun. Next time I'm bringing Maho," referring to her stuffed raccoon.

I was more anxious all the time. The feeling reached the point where it was sometimes hard to breathe.

A week passed, then a month passed, and then two.

I was such a nervous wreck about my sister that I practically begged her, telling her repeatedly that she was not allowed to go back to the place. She didn't listen. It was like she got a kick out of seeing me like this.

If she wasn't there when I got home from school, I lost my mind. I had to leave the house to look for her. But when I made it to the secret place, she wasn't there. Had she fallen? My legs trembled and turned to jelly. Looking over the cliff, I saw no sign of her. Each time I went home in a daze, only to find her there ahead of me. This gave me the distinct feeling of a heavy object passing down my throat. I became afraid of choking on my food, each piece turning into dead weight after I had swallowed, like it was stuck there, so that I had to take these tiny little bites. When I came to my senses, my heart was running wild. I tossed and turned and tried lying on my side, but my heartbeat pounded through the bed, booming in the ear I pressed into the pillow.

This gave rise to a peculiar sensation. Attempting now to put it into words, I suppose it would be something like this:

The torment wouldn't end until my sister fell off of the cliff.

This isn't what I wanted. But the disturbing,

sticky question of when my sister was going to fall must have driven me to think up a solution. I didn't care what happened, as long as it meant ending this anxiety, in whatever shape or form.

Which is why I thanked her when my sister asked if we could go again and promised that she wasn't going back alone. I knew that she had gone back there alone, but I suspect that she had sensed the threat outside our door and wanted me beside her. Later on, it came to light that someone had killed themself up there a while back. A young man tortured by an impossible love, who took his own life in a sentimental fashion. Perhaps what drew us to the place was a signaturely juvenile desire to find a secret hideaway, an early gesture of rebellion against our parents, common enough for kids our age. Though looking back, I'm not so sure.

My sister took along Maho the stuffed raccoon. It was a Sunday evening. We had to be home before dark.

Once we got there, she was hyper, like she was up to some kind of mischief. Sitting Maho the raccoon down beside her, she announced that we were going to play house.

Me and my sister were husband and wife, and Maho the raccoon was our daughter. It bothered me having my secret place turned into a house. I was in third grade, for crying out loud. Playing house with her tended to go on forever, and we had to make it home by dark, so I refused—knowing that she couldn't tell on me to Grandma. She started crying, turned her back on me and told me to go home. But when she said that next time she was coming back alone, my throat bunched up and I felt like I couldn't breathe again. The anxiety was back. Hoping to calm her down, I approached her from behind. My sister had her back to me, but her stuffed raccoon stared me down. This grubby stuffed raccoon, however powerless, was threatening me. I asked myself why I would find it threatening. This thing was a stuffed animal; it couldn't warn my sister that I was coming closer. For whatever reason, that was what was on my mind. As I approached, I came up with the idea of surprising her. That would teach her just how dangerous a place this was. Probably stop her from coming back. If suddenly I grabbed her by the shoulders, I could scare her and keep her safe at the same time, since I'd be holding on to her. In my mind, it felt like I was watching a black string, loosely tangled and unraveling. My hands were almost on my sister. The lump thickened in my throat, and to my surprise, my heart sped up. The tip of the black string frayed, branching off, until finally, before my very eyes, it blended with the bulky, overlapping shafts of shadow and the geometric patterns that had shown up on the floor at the funeral. A town lamenting the death of a young girl. A father and mother embracing, shaken by the death of a young girl. Something made these images come back to me. My pulse was screaming, as if to warn me of the danger. Reaching out, I grabbed my sister's tiny shoulder with my right hand. As soon as I did, I felt a strange sensation in all five fingers. Like I had touched something I never should have touched. My sister whipped my hand away, and in the same motion she let go of the raccoon.

Losing her balance trying to grab it, my skinny little sister's left foot slipped and she went skidding down the cliff. I watched her in a daze. She had made all of these movements on her own, as I watched. Watching her fall, as if experiencing the inevitable, I felt the lump go down my throat and disappear.

Why did I bring my sister up there in the first place? I know inside of me, I had a guilty conscience for having hit her. I mean, I know I never hit her, but in my own childish way, this deviant guilt persisted. Which made me unopposed to bringing her along, as an apology. If my intentions had been murderous, I'm sure I would have been too scared to bring her, coward that I am. There was something odd about my guilty conscience. Almost like I felt the guilt for having murdered her, but in advance, and brought her to the place trying to make up for it, in a bizarre mental loop.

My outlandish drumming heart would not stop beating. What had made me tell my sister so persistently to stay away from there, knowing all too well that it would make her do the opposite?

My bright idea, hatched by my third grader brain, was to surprise her. Could a kid as young as me have harbored such a seething murderous intent? Either way, the real problem was the outcome of my actions. I heard a voice. "Somebody must have pushed her." The voice of the character on the anime I always watched. And that somebody who had pushed her was unquestionably me.

My legs went weak. I was unable to move, much less let emit a breath, or breathe one in, or use my voice. I crouched down, ready to go to sleep then and there. But the voice from the anime would not relent. Just kept on talking. This is what it said.

"If it wasn't you who pushed her, your life is about to get even worse."

Looking up from the pages, I saw the cigarette that I left burning in the ashtray. I had forgotten all about it. It had burned down to the filter before I had a chance to take a puff.

Outside the window, the trees were dancing in their disagreeable manner, somehow looking closer than before. Like unholy pendulums. It was long after dark.

I returned my attention to the manuscript. It wasn't all that long. I'd probably read about a third of it.

These words were lonesome. At least to me. Why? Because the majority of people would be at a loss to sympathize with them. The odd one out is cast away. In that sense, Kozuka's story was similar to my own.

What did I think? A grin formed on my lips. In a certain sense, I had no sympathy for him. Why? Because I rarely experienced anything deserving of the word emotion. The most that happened is my heart fluttered a bit sometimes. A relic of my emotive past, if you will. Flipping a bit ahead, I picked up the word "sister" and found she had survived with injuries, but my only thought was "Oh, I guess she didn't die."

I glanced at the white suitcase in the corner. The pages before my eyes that recounted his life story—*a lifetime wrapped into a package.*

Though only partway through, I reflected on what I had read thus far. This had been a dismal life.

Right, I thought. *That explains why his life cost me almost nothing.*

I felt something rising up inside of me, moving upward in a spiral. Before I could coax it any higher, I swallowed it down. I had a headache. I tried to slow my speeding heart down with deep breaths. I looked around me. I had to think. Now that I had Kozuka's identity, I had to disappear and soon.

I lit another cigarette and read on. Two-thirds to go.

My sister didn't die. Tumbling down the cliff, her body took a beating, spinning out of control, but a pile of abandoned tires and wrecked bicycles caught her fall. She was unconscious, both legs broken and a dislocated shoulder, but not mortally wounded. A fall like that should certainly have killed her, but chance got in the way. A group of kids collecting bugs nearby discovered her.

Later, I found out that the punishments for murder and attempted murder differed. This meant that punishment was not determined solely on a person's murderous intentions and behavior. Strange how in the end, my punishment had been commuted by a stroke of fortune. Changed by fortune of a kind the human brain cannot detect, factors surpassing human intellect.

Everything changed at home. The event was called an accident, but that didn't change the fact I'd tried to kill her. I lacked a framework to explain the workings of my inner world, and even if I could I'm sure they would have been reduced to murder. Grandma made herself sick, and Dad became so angry he abandoned any of his scruples about smacking Mom in the face. Cheeks and left eye all puffed up, she wound up taking me away from there. She had a fracture in the bone of her left arm and tied it up with bandages. My psychological transgression against my little sister had resulted in my mother's puffy cheeks and fractured arm. Just as I had caused the twitch in Grandma's eye, I was the swelling in my mother's cheeks, and was the fracture in her arm. Soon Grandma died.

Mom moved us back to her hometown, a Tokyo suburb where her parents had already died, and started working as a hostess. My mom's dad had evidently been quite the drinker, and my mom drank too. When something upsetting happened at the bar, she drank even more. One time she asked me to my face, "Do I honestly deserve this?" I get what she was saying. It was bad luck that her second husband was so violent. To me my sister was only half related, but without a doubt she was my mother's daughter. This made all the difference between my mom and me. What I had done frightened me to no end. If it hadn't been for a coincidence, fact is I would have been a murderer. It was a matter of the act not being realized, though I was sure that it was out there, existing as its own separate thing. And while I failed to grasp this thing that I felt moving around deep inside of me, I had a vague sense of something being out of place. "Do I honestly deserve this?" I couldn't help but wish that instead of asking me, she could have asked this thing that was inside of me.

It didn't take long for Mom to bring a customer home from the bar. Sometimes this guy punched her. More often than not, the violence just beyond the fusuma transitioned into sexual intercourse. The apartment we had moved into was cramped, just two rooms and a kitchen.

The fusuma in my room was even ricketier than the door at the old house. Usually they kicked me out of the apartment beforehand, but sometimes they started going at it with me right there. Things got relatively peaceful when this guy stopped coming by, though Mom did spend a lot more time in front of the scuzzy exhaust fan, smoking cigarettes and spacing out. Then some other guy who punched Mom made himself at home. The guys who didn't punch mom never stuck around for long.

My mom was lonely. How come the men she brought home had to be abusive? How come the men who weren't abusive never stayed? At the time I lacked the resources to analyze the situation.

The guy who lived with us around the time I entered the fourth grade beat me too. He was a leftie and mostly used his palm, though sometimes he kicked me using his left foot. When this happened, my mom would cry and beg for him to stop, but when he did he always dragged her into the next room so he could beat her up instead. Sometimes this became sex, and through the fusuma I heard my mother's voice, surfacing despite attempts to stifle it. My response to this was to play video games. Back then this meant the "Family Computer" from Nintendo. Contrary to the name, no one used the thing but me. I immersed myself in video games. Pretty soon I did the same with anime and manga. I suppose they were a place where I could construct a world all my own.

In *Super Mario Bros.*, the character named Mario, along with Luigi in two-player mode, fights to rescue Princess Peach, who's been captured by a turtle monster named King Koopa. Uninterested in rescuing the Princess, I lingered in the levels, declining to use the warps provided in the game, so that I could remain in each world as long as possible. Enemies appeared. I dodged them repeatedly, jumping up to squash them every time. Other games were popular by then, but this was the only game I owned, since it had come with my used Nintendo. Once I started something, I was capable of focusing obsessively forever. But through the goofy music of the game, I could hear my mother's voice. And when I was watching *Dragon Ball*, and the main character, Goku, blew his stack fighting a bad guy, her voice was audible too.

Something happened that same year, when I was in the fourth grade, on a clear day just before summer vacation. I was walking along, annoyed at how the inside of the right foot of my gym shoes always wore out faster. Partway down the straight shot between school and home, I looked up to find a grownup woman walking ahead of me, wearing a short skirt. Those long legs, skin so white and soft, looked almost squishy, especially what I could see of her bare thighs. At the sight of them, my penis got insanely big.

This became a regular thing. It started happening when I heard my mom's voice through the music of the video games or anime. It made me worried, so I pushed my way through by sinking even deeper into whatever was onscreen. But this only made my penis bigger, so big it started hurting, until I sensed a lure of pleasure I had never felt before. Really worried now, I tried to picture Mario or Goku. I focused on images of Mario in midair or Goku fighting, in an attempt to cover up the woman's legs I saw before me. But Mario and Goku were as good as weightless. Scattering helplessly, torn apart like paper, only for the legs to reappear, whiter than ever.

What the hell was going on? My penis rubbed against my jeans when I was walking, which made the pleasant feeling more acute. Going around with all these feelings in my head, I started walking up to women. Their perfume streamed into my body. I'm sure these women had no clue their perfume was having this effect on kids. If only I could touch those legs. They had a power over me which it was thoroughly clear that I was ill-equipped to handle. Feeling so good I was woozy, I wondered about bumping into them. Like, if I bumped into them accidentally, I could apologize. No, that would be wrong. It was wrong to do a thing like that.

I tried sorting out my thoughts, but I got the sense that it was better for me to direct this bizarre feeling in my penis toward the women I saw, rather than toward my mother. Should I just go with it? Who should I direct this feeling at? My thoughts tied themselves in knots. I walked quickly, unable to slow down. I had no way of dispatching this new excitement. Wondering if I could just bump into them, just like that, I gently bumped into a woman's leg. That moment, the good feeling broke the boundaries of permissibility; I got woozy, wanting even more. My penis brushed against her leg, and when I felt the softness, enveloped by the sweet stimulation of her perfume, I experienced semenarche.

Women might not be familiar with this term. Semenarche is the first time that a man ejaculates. In most cases, it happens to boys in the fifth or sixth grade, leaving them confused about the source of their erections and why this white fluid comes out when their penis feels good. Not realizing its relation to sexuality, lots of boys worry that they're sick, concerned something unusual is happening to them.

I should have been found out by society then and there. A group of adults could have looked into my family history, met to formulate a strategy, and set about fixing my head. But the woman went so easy on me. At a loss for words, she looked back at me aghast. At the miserable schoolkid who had just brushed up against her leg and ejaculated in his pants. Though I don't think the woman realized I had come. Dopey kid I was, she may have even thought that I was "special needs." All she said was this: *"Never do that again."* The slanting rays of sunlight caught my body. The woman started saying something else but hesitated, seemingly afraid, and walked away, leaving the smell of her perfume. It felt like she had abandoned me, left me crumpled in a heap on the asphalt.

In that moment, I genuinely felt "abandoned." I felt provoked by the uneventful nature of the world around me, though I had witnessed changes in my body and behavior. Was the timing of the semenarche a coincidence? Hard to say. As a result of my transgression against my sister, my stifling life had changed. It might have been worse than before, but at the very least, I had found myself in different circumstances. I must have realized I could use violence to attempt to change my circumstances. Otherwise, why else would I feel "provoked by the uneventful nature of the world"? My pants were filthy. I looked around repeatedly, making sure I didn't see any of my classmates, and went home feeling a mix of shame, pleasure, and horror. As selfish as it was, maybe I had wished that woman could have taken me away somewhere.

You're probably wondering if I repeated this behavior, walking around town in search of the same pleasure. But that was the first time and the last. Semenarche gave way to abstinence. Was this an error?

Late one night, around the time I started the fifth grade, my drunk mom gave me a warning.

I was still abstaining. My mom and some guy were going at it. In an attempt to make them stop, I slid open the fusuma, pretending I was heading to the bathroom. They were moving underneath the comforter, so I didn't see them doing it exactly. After the guy went home all crestfallen, Mom ranked on me for always staying up too late, for being good at nothing but my schoolwork and forgetting things all of the time. Totally unrelated stuff. Her breath was a mixture of alcohol and the simmered meat we had for dinner. My head began to hurt. In an attempt to get her to stop talking, I gave her a little push. Because my mom was drunk, she threw her arms up and crashed against the wall, way harder than I'd pushed her. She had always had a habit of playing up how hurt she was.

There she was, my masochistic mother, back against the wall. But what caught my eye was something else. For a split second, it looked like she was tempting me, as if by force of habit.

When men beat up my mom, it was common for her and these guys to start having sex. The violence not only led into sex; it had an inherently sexual component. On top of all of that, I suppose my mom was acting out of self-preservation, encouraging the men to have sex so that they would stop beating her. She was trying to protect herself from further pain. And without realizing, Mom had done the same to me. For a split second, she had looked like she was making eyes at me, like she was pressing on the driving force of sexuality inside of me, provoking me to act. A faint smile appeared on her lips. I don't think she meant to do it. But after I had pushed her, she started looking at me like that without realizing. In that instant, something tore me asunder. All the men who had punched Mom cascaded into me. I felt the high of blowing past my weaker self, the chance to move from being hit into the one doing the hitting. Except I couldn't bring myself to do it. She was a woman. How could I punch my mom? Much less do something sexual, knowing I was unable to control myself. Everything that I had bottled up inside of me came gushing out. I grabbed a shelf that had been pulled loose from the cupboard by the guy when he was beating

Mom and slammed it down onto the kitchen island, where we kept the kettle and the frying pans. Again I thought that I could see the same black string, tip branching off and aimlessly unraveling. I swung the shelf down over and over again, so that my hands were screaming and shed blood. Shards of broken plates flew through the air at Mom. She cowered at me from the floor. It had not been my intention to shower her with broken plates. Much less for my pent-up violence to be manifested in the shards. When I saw blood dripping from her cheek, it was actually a relief. A sensation filled my body, like I had finally gotten what I wanted, like all that had been bottled up had finally been released, after so many years. Blood flushed my cheeks. A warmness spread around my heart and neck. But I felt sorry for my mom and stumbled to her. Flooded all at once with every possible emotion, I felt so dizzy that I had to take a seat beside her.

This is when I was found out by society. My panic-stricken mother told on me. The scorn she harbored toward me must have made her do it. Besides, without having me around, she was free to go back to her old house and live with her daughter. Maybe she blamed me, at a level so profoundly deep she failed to notice, for things always going so poorly with those men.

At my age, it would be difficult to put me into juvenile hall, but that wasn't really on the table. I was deemed emotionally unstable and sent off to what we now call a residential treatment center for troubled youth, where they fixed my head. Once I was out, my mom refused to take me back, too scared to be around me, so I moved into a children's home until they found some other grownups to take me.

. . . It doesn't even feel like this is me. It's all so blurry, like something shrouded in a distant fog. But evidently somebody is going to take my place. Someone willing to take over for me, accepting all the horrors . . . I'm going to be saved.

My hand stopped flipping through the pages. Less than a quarter left.

A person who would take his place? Accepting all the horrors . . . ?

Once there was a man named Tsutomu Miyazaki.

I doubt there's anyone in Japan around my

age who doesn't know about him. He was one of the most infamous criminals in Japan. In the space of a year, starting in 1988, he murdered four young girls. This was around the time that I was living in the treatment center. Miyazaki was sentenced to death by the Supreme Court in 2006 and executed on June 17th, 2008.

He was known as the "Otaku Murderer." The owner of nearly six thousand tapes of anime and other movies and a vast collection of manga, he played with the genitalia of the girls he murdered and consumed their remains. The incidents spread use of the word *otaku* far and wide. These acts were dismissed as the doings of a twisted pedophile, hopelessly mired in fictional worlds, but when I dug deeper, I saw something else was going on.

Miyazaki had a hereditary disability called bilateral congenital radioulnar synostosis, which prevented him from rotating his palms up. In practice, he was unable to cup his hands the way we do when we're receiving something small, like change after a purchase. This meant that he could hand things over, but he couldn't easily accept them.

He was a quiet kid, easy to miss. The adult couples in his family were at odds with one another, and sometimes his grandfather beat his grandmother and his father beat his mother. Because his parents were both busy working, he was looked after by a man named Taka, who had an emotional disorder and was unable to use both his legs. After Taka went away and Miyazaki's grandfather died, a noticeable change came over him. He began inflicting violence on his parents and on animals while obsessively collecting anime and manga.

Children can become unstable with the death of a parent or close relative, but by the time his grandfather had died Miyazaki was already twenty-five years old and inordinately distraught. When he saw a little girl on her own, he told himself "I'm gonna catch that kid" and said something to her. Of particular interest was his perception of himself during that moment.

When Miyazaki walked off with a girl, he said he felt like he was watching it happen from behind, as a person similar to him led the girl away. That person, however, was the same height as the girl. What follows is an explanation, in his own words.

"The world outside was terrifying, and I always had a prickly feeling in my heart, but sometimes a mysterious force would suddenly give me an order, increasing the terror in a way I couldn't shake. If I ignored the order I was scared I would be lynched or worse, so in order to obey the orders (there were many) I'd start walking, but it was another me who walked ahead (without looking back at me), which told me that this other me was also following the orders of these mysterious forces. It made my heart beat out of control, out of terror and disgust, but the other me bumbled ahead. As if he had no sensory perception whatsoever." [from letter]

In such a state, Miyazaki led the girl to a forest

that he had fond memories of visiting on a picnic years ago. The girl began to scream.

"She started screaming. Realizing I was betrayed, I became frightened and begged myself not to attack her, getting more and more scared, until things went out of control. I can't remember the rest. Ten or so of these guys the size of grownups, but with faces like rats, surrounded me." [from testimony]

Creatures with the faces of rats. Sometimes he called them "Rat Men." As soon as the girl cried out, the Rat Men surrounded Miyazaki. To stop the girl from crying, he strangled her to death, though he didn't think he was the one who did it. After the murder, he fled the scene. When he went back the next day, the girl's body was still there.

The fact that there was not one Rat Man but rather several has been totally overlooked, but I see this as the most important thing.

Why more than one? My sense is that it came

from being bullied during school, along with his terror of society as a whole. His history of being bullied was a fact. As a kid, he described schools for only girls or only boys as having "one kind of humans" and coed schools as "having two kinds of humans." Preferring the first option, he went to a school for boys, but said that his experience with bullying was "excessive and relentless." Unlike most otaku, his preferences in anime and monster movies were limited to what he liked when he was younger. In other words, his psychological world was an attempt to remain in childhood.

Though it pained him to do so, he eventually started to record the grownup shows he had no interest in. Asked why he filmed all these shows—back to back, no space between them—he said that it was so the outside world had no way in. He was attempting to construct a safe zone around himself.

First he lost Taka, who had doted on him like he was a child, and then he lost his grandfather, who saw him as a grandson, meaning as a child, no matter his age. With this death, his psychological world and safe zone crumbled. Now that he needed strength the most, he felt the pressure to conform. In the process, he was haunted by the years of bullying he had endured, progressively intensifying from elementary school through middle school and high school. He says his tendency to lash out at his parents came from a conviction that his parents were going to attack him. He had to get back to his childhood. Had to reinforce it. His sexual impulses were undeveloped, falling short of thoughts of penetration (he was a virgin), but this was only because his psychological experience was stuck in childhood, and the death of his grandfather kicked his stunted sex drive into gear. Shoring up his childhood made him dependent on others. Others who would regard him as a child. The shorter version of himself, walking off with the girl, was obviously him as a child. But the girl started to cry. In that instant, he felt betrayed, and the world of his childhood came crashing down. Beyond the falling walls, the "bullying" awaited him. He was surrounded by the Rat Men. He had to do something to prevent total collapse. The Rat Men were going to lynch him. Stop crying, please stop crying. That was when he killed the girl.

Afterward, he sacrificed her to the resurrection of his grandfather, but first he stripped her body of her clothes. He says he watched a person who resembled him stripping the clothes off the body, from a vantage point diagonally behind them. By his account, he couldn't really see what this person was doing.

Throughout the court proceedings, the results of various psychiatric examinations were released: "personality disorder," "schizophrenia," "dissociative identity disorder (multiple personality disorder)." The results were inconclusive. My guess is this was probably because he had been removed from the context that had been so formative to his condition and been dropped into unfamiliar circumstances. Furthermore, this was the first appearance of "dissociative identity disorder" in a trial in Japan, and the pathology had (shockingly) yet to achieve widespread recognition in the Japanese psychiatric medicine community.

You can talk about this incident from all sorts of different angles, but my interest is the Rat Men. What people need to recognize is why someone otherwise so timid was able to murder these girls.

Consider his personality at the time he murdered the girl. Clearly something was happening out of sync with his timid self. The girl starts crying, he's surrounded by the Rat Men, he experiences terror. Feels compelled to make this girl who won't stop crying "disappear." That much adds up. But reason would suggest he would have acted like a coward. Surrounded by the Rat Men, you would have thought he would have crawled into a ball in terror and lost consciousness. Allowing the girl to escape. That would have made a lot more sense. And yet he murdered her. Not an easy thing to do. So what allowed for him to murder her like that?

Miyazaki was executed in 2008. When they

looped the rope around his neck to hang him, they say he was obliging. Whoever he had been when he had killed the girls had disappeared somewhere inside his mind, and in the moment of his execution, he did nothing. You could say this was the person who had watched the murders happen. The person who had done the watching was the person who they executed. Society had demanded capital punishment, but it was unable to execute the person who had killed the girl, instead looping the noose around the neck of an apathetic man whose world was blank.

Uppermost Drawer

The account ended abruptly.

I was surprised. Why would somebody stop there? Hardly a good place to stop. Rat Men? What did this have to do with Ryodai Kozuka?

A little piece of paper stuck to the last page said "Uppermost Drawer." That must be where the rest of it was hidden.

Sure enough, the desk had three drawers. No choice but to check them. I opened the first drawer.

Nothing. So I checked the second, and then the third, and gasped. My heart sped up. Along with two more old sheets of paper, same size as what I'd read, I found a key.

A rudimentary key like this could only be for a suitcase.

A doorbell rang out of nowhere. I felt a dull pang in my heart. I looked at the door, whose lumber was decrepit as the paper. But then I got the feeling I had heard the same bell earlier, except farther away. This time it was the neighboring room.

Someone was ringing all the doorbells in the lodge, working their way down the rooms. Each time a little closer. Who would venture this far out into the woods? Whoever they were, if they went around back, the light from the window would give me away. Lights out. Outside the window, the dark trees felt like they were closing in on me.

Given such a choice, how is one to proceed? I chose the suitcase. Why? Because the keyhole of the suitcase looked too tempting. I remembered something similar from the account. Except it was about a door. *Open it, and my entire life could transform in an instant.* I tried the key, a perfect fit, and turned. The latch unlocked.

It was a corpse. My field of vision narrowed. The dead body of an adult in a fetal position, wrapped in a thick transparent plastic bag. It was a woman.

So what made Miyazaki capable of murdering the girl? Analyzing the crime in simple terms, using the sort of logic attempted above, won't get us anywhere. Let's go straight to the heart of the matter. What follows is my best attempt at using language, unlike anyone before me, to delve into the complexities of human psychology. Deep into the interior experience of a criminal, the recesses of a mind.

Bereft of the sanctuary of Taka and his grandfather, this man of twenty-five, who feared the world around him, was confronted with a little girl. I wrote earlier of how he told himself, "I'm gonna catch that kid." Judging from the circumstances, it would follow he was answering to the commands (or voices) of the Rat Men, but that calls one thing into question.

Being commanded to take action would surely have been disagreeable. Why did the Rat Men need to force him into doing something that "appealed" to him?

Miyazaki likely told himself "I'm gonna catch that kid" as soon as he saw the girl, without provocation from the Rat Men. But he would have recognized that doing so would be a deviation from social custom. The thought of "catching the girl" would have paralyzed him with anxiety. An anxiety which transcended its content and took on a generic form, reflexively summoning the Rat Men.

The Rat Men existed to command. In that moment, Miyazaki was already inclined to "take the girl away." The Rat Men had simply latched onto his inclinations and bid him to proceed. In effect, this would mean that *Miyazaki used the Rat Men as a tool*. Coward that he was, he could never have done something so appalling unless someone had commanded him. My guess is the bullies in his school years must have forced him into doing a large number of things he never could have otherwise done. Though out of fear, he followed through on what they ordered him to do. If given the command, he was capable of taking off his clothes in front of people, or of shoplifting. In the realms of his unconscious, this transformed into a pathology, to the point where he was able to approach the girl and lead her off by processing the action as a "command."

That made it no less terrifying for him. Which is why he became detached and saw himself at a remove, watching a child version of himself from behind, walking with the girl. While he had always felt disconnected from his life to some degree, being bullied or experiencing life at its most painful moments often forced him to disconnect from his feelings entirely, a fatal pattern of response that soon entrenched itself in his perception of the world. Whoever was around him disappeared, and he discovered himself in a blissful landscape where he played as a child. Judging from the testimony, at times like this he would migrate from the self watching from behind into the self beside the girl. However frightened he had been initially, once he had cleared the hurdle of "catching the girl" and was no longer worried about anybody seeing him, he no longer had a reason to disconnect.

Then the girl cries. He feels betrayed. Here is where the Rat Men surround him. As I wrote earlier, this is the result of the disintegration he experienced in childhood, but at the same time, he was experiencing the terror of a child crying, a terror he could not accept; a scathing terror, as a result of which the cry was processed as an attack. The terror and the Rat Men are connected. To make the emergent Rat Men go away, he first would need to address the sources of his terror and anxiety. He had to shut the girl up. That much he knew. But what made him capable of murdering her? The answer has to do with a number of problems tormenting Miyazaki.

In elementary school, he had murdered a small pet bird in a fit of hatred, but after burying the thing regretted his behavior, dug it up, and stroked it as he cried. He said that he had also killed bugs on occasion, but that the idea was to help them, since their past lives had prevented them from being born again as humans. I suspect, however, that the disability of his hands adds another layer. The hatred that he felt was both toward the society that disregarded him and toward himself, and found an outlet on those bugs and on the bird. In a sense it was a kind of vicarious suicide, in which his yearning to be reborn in a different life found substitute.

When his grandfather died, the desire to deny that it had happened was intense, and the boundary between life and death became so blurred he had delusions of his grandfather coming back to life.

There were also episodes where Miyazaki only managed to take a picture of a girl, because she had resisted and escaped. He killed the girls when they were so alone "he felt like no one else existed," to the point where the little girl was no longer another person (or an individual, which Miyazaki defined as someone who would do him harm). If this perception fell apart (when a girl fought back and cried), thus revealing the girl's "individuality," Miyazaki experienced a chaotic anger, furious about her breaking things apart.

His anger was that of an eruptive personality that had surfaced in the midst of his return to childhood, a temporary shift to a ferocious personality, lacking in reason like that of a child, and characterized by its detachment— perhaps not in the sense of a clean break, but rather something partial, as if only from the elbows upward. This "break" was helpful in two ways: in yielding the perception of him being "disconnected" from the person who was attempting the murder, and in prompting the terror of him being lynched by the Rat Men, were he to disobey. He converted this terror into the *courage* to commit the murder, on the reasoning that it was kill or be killed. Meanwhile, he persistently exhibited an abnormal interest in the "death" that had besieged his grandfather. The death that had deprived him of what mattered to him most. It had been torn away from him. But what about the other way around? What if he became a "doer," taking death into his own hands? Would this bring him closer to a mastery over death? Would death become less scary than it was before? I have mentioned his intention to sacrifice the girls to the realm of his grandfather, but there was also the possibility that he perceived these acts as a way to become more familiar with the passage between life and death, allowing it to widen. Murder—the enormity of this atrocious deed was lessened by the use of words like *sacrifice*. Above all, there must have been a drive to erase the "individuality" of the girl. Because to Miyazaki, "individuality" (with respect to other people or society) had always been a horrible and hateful thing.

It would seem that all of these things happened in an instant, more or less simultaneously. Taking advantage of his feelings of "disconnection" and "the pressures of his terror of the Rat Men," he recast himself as a victim, giving rise to a separate personality who could then strangle the girl. His experience of seeing his grandfather beat his grandmother, and his father beat his mother, played a role, along with his experiences of being beaten. He had spent more of his life near violence than the average person. This had taught him lessons, unconsciously *encouraging* him to think that having this violence inside of him, along with the potential that it held, would surely make him capable of doing these things too. Most likely, the motivation to capture/photograph each girl as an object arose after she was killed.

He did not recall the criminal act of strangling the girl as something he had done himself.

It all seemed like a dream. The next day, he went back to where it happened. As he had made no attempt to hide the body, it was where he had left it. He did the same thing three more times before he was arrested. His primary objective was probably to create a world of childhood together with the girl "once and for all," and if that proved to be impossible, he likely thought that he could murder and thus "capture" her. There is the possibility that the brutal cycle of emotions—girl cries, Rat Men close in—had embedded itself in his psyche and demanded repetition. Brutal experiences urge people to repeat them. The endogenous opioids secreted by our brain to quell our terror and discomfort have been known to be released, in certain cases, at such levels that a person can essentially become addicted to the solace they provide. In some cases, they can even provide the solace of having dodged a crisis.

Miyazaki could not, however, capture the girls as they had actually lived. For someone as immersed in visual media as him, images

held greater sway than reality. And so he pho-
tographed their corpses, so he could capture
the images. Since he was too scared to remove
their clothes and look at them, he became
detached and looked on from behind. *But
even he could handle the photographic images.
The perspective they afforded was impersonal,
lacking individuality*—as a result of which his
undeveloped sexuality was set in motion, in
its undeveloped state. As goes without saying,
sexual behavior urges repetition. On the whole,
his sexuality was greatly influenced by his
obsessive "hoarding." Even the tamest among
us, if subjected to attacks from society or other
people—or if, in the parlance of this example,
we allow the Rat Men to infiltrate our body—
has the potential to become a criminal. When
Miyazaki crossed the line, in a certain sense he
flung himself into the arms of the Rat Men.

There is a possibility that his experience of the
"Rat Men" was a delusional recollection, formed
after he had been arrested and placed in a

strange environment—a possibility he had created them after the fact, in the psychiatric state
that we call custody. But even if that were the
case, the end result would be that he had taken
this behavior, which "made no sense" to him at
the time, and portrayed it later using a childish
cast of characters (the Rat Men). Taken that
which he could not verbalize, and subsequently
used the Rat Men to explain it, as a narrative.
To repeat, the Rat Men can be understood as a
concoction of the gaze of the entire world mixed
with the horrors promised by society.

Following his arrest, Miyazaki talked about
his experience with bullying, but no one was
assigned to investigate or analyze the details,
leaving this factor wholly unexplored. But I
believe that herein lies the hidden kernel of
the case—that in his history of being bullied,
something sexual happened. This would tell
us everything we need to know about the gen-
esis of his motives, which have thus far been
regarded as a mystery.

My belief is that he committed the crimes when he was on the brink of dissociative identity disorder and moved further into that condition around the time of his arrest, until finally he denied the allegations, having infantilized himself in an unconscious act of self-protection (his remarks gradually became incoherent). Not only was he still a virgin, but he had also never pulled back his foreskin, though his intelligence was normal, and no sperm had been detected on the bodies of the girls or in his room. Such was his detachment from sex (not the looking and touching kind, but insertion and ejaculation). The testimony notes a history with masturbation, though no mention of whether he ever ejaculated. He said his sexual fantasies involved imagining himself as a kid and straddling the horizontal bar, remembering how good it felt. No one else around. One source of dissociative identity disorder is sexual abuse. Returning to the "eruptive personality" mentioned earlier, in many cases people with dissociative identity disorder will reassign their "angry" feelings to a separate personality (the physical embodiment of anger). I think there is a very high probability that Miyazaki was a victim of sexual abuse or harassment. It makes you wonder what kind of lives the guys who bullied him are living now. There was also a high probability that the bullying was in actuality rather slight, but had bloated in the context of his paranoia. A kick in the testicles or a laugh about the size of his penis could have been blown out of proportion—

And so he was executed. With no true grasp of his role in what he had done.

To whoever reads these words . . . What are you feeling as you read them? I'm thankful for your time. But I'm afraid that it may be too late for you . . . YOU'D BETTER RUN.

Once again, the account ended abruptly.

Tsutomu Miyazaki? Rat Men? I could care less about all that. It was none of my concern. All I wanted to know was why there was a woman's body in the suitcase.

YOU'D BETTER RUN.

What was that about? Was this guy collecting

criminal case studies? Why? To what end? Now what was I supposed to—

The bell again. My heart sped up so fast it hurt. This time the bell was clearly for this room. I looked at the body of the woman in the suitcase and turned my eyes back to the door.

Without making a sound, I shut the suitcase and hid it underneath the bed, then locked the door. I'd better sit tight for a while. Except I couldn't think of anything else. The knob rattled the door. Something slipped into the lock and it released. A pain shot through my heart. I knew I had to run, but I just stood there, unable to move. It felt like the trees outside the window were working their way in. The door opened.

The dim light from outside swung through the darkness of the room. It was a man. Shoulders wet, he looked at me, expressionless.

Seconds passed, what felt like minutes. My throat went dry.

"What is it?" I asked him. That was all that I could say. The expressionless man held his gaze. He wore a black jacket and looked like he was in his forties.

"Feel okay?" he finally asked.

"About what?"

"Never mind . . . forget it. Let's get out of here. We'd better hurry."

The man gave me an umbrella. A worn-out plastic umbrella. I thought about the suitcase under the bed. I couldn't just leave it there.

"Wait, I just . . ."

"Look, we can't talk here. The place . . . is bugged."

"What?"

The man pressed a finger to his lips. A thin finger.

"Not now. Hurry up."

I followed him outside, opening the umbrella. He led me to an expensive-looking car, white but not recently washed.

"We can talk inside. Time to get out of here."

The door to the back seat opened. Once I was in, the man sat in the driver's seat. The seatbelt felt oddly tight against my waist. I tried to adjust it but the belt wouldn't unlock.

". . . I'm not interested in grappling with you in the rain."

The man spoke without looking back.

"Huh?"

"Take a load off . . . Ryodai Kozuka."

I let out a breath. This was unbelievable.

"What are you talking about? You're confused . . . All right, I'll explain everything."

"This again . . . Let me guess, you're not Ryodai Kozuka. You really are a stubborn guy, you know that?"

This was not okay. But the belt wouldn't unbuckle. I was stuck there.

"Listen, okay? I'm not Kozuka . . . it's a long story, let me explain. I changed my identity—"

"Identity?"

"Yeah. I changed identities. Trading places with Ryodai Kozuka."

"Trade places? How?"

"I needed a new identity, okay? This is what I wound up getting . . ."

"Got yourself a new identity, huh . . . Amazing."

I tried unbuckling the belt.

"It's not like that. I know what you're trying to say. But back in that room, you can read all about this Kozuka guy you're looking for. A whole stack of pages."

"Yeah," the driver said, driving along. "Written by you."

I let out another breath. This idiocy was unaccept-
able. What a pompous asshole.

"That's not it. Let me explain from the beginning
. . . just let me out, okay?" I kicked the back of the
driver's seat. "Did you expect me to just sit here quietly?
Do yourself a favor and quit messing around."

". . . We have a letter. Though in all likelihood you
sent the thing yourself. Care to read it?"

". . . A letter?"

"I bet you're going to say this isn't you either. But it's
too late for you to escape."

First off, I owe you a sincere apology.

*If you're reading this, a man is taking you
away, instead of Ryodai Kozuka. Those guys are
probably convinced that's who you are. They think
you're delusional for insisting that you're not
Kozuka when, at least to them, you are.*

*That sort of thing might work in movies or in
manga, but it won't fly in real life. Obviously you
have a different face, and they have to understand
that plastic surgery can only go so far. I need you
to relax. The misunderstanding will be cleared up*

at the hospital. They have his DNA on file there. There's no way it could match yours. So for now, go along with it. Don't give the guy who picked you up a hard time.

I'm sure you're wondering why you should go along with this. But it's a long story, and this is just one part. *You may as well relax. They'll admit you for a little while but you'll be out of there in no time. All you have to do is sit in for Kozuka for a week, until the results of the DNA test come through.*

6

Emerging from the ill-lit mountain road, we could see a rundown hospital in the distance. It appeared to be two floors, but overall was not so very large, barely making an impression on the darkness.

It was a long way back to town. Perhaps the city lights could be seen from the hospital, but I suspect it would be hard to see the hospital from town. No one would notice if the building disappeared. The trees danced, as if alerting me once more to something sinister.

The ashen concrete walls, which seemed to have distended from the ground, looked horribly askew. We entered the hospital through what must have been the rear entrance, a glass door smeared with fingerprints. My head hurt. The man led us down a narrow hall. Simple light fixtures and excessively thick doors. Perhaps from all the rain outside, everything I saw looked wet. It felt like the coolness emanating from the walls and hallway amplified our footsteps.

". . . Where are we going?"

"To the see the doctor."

The hallway ended at a white door. It was as if doors were all I saw, likely the result of reading Kozuka's account. The man opened the door and stepped aside, remaining by the threshold while I went in. The room was small. Strange pictures on the walls and an ancient, scrawny desk lamp. He left me in there with a different man, a doctor, who sat behind the desk and looked at me, wearing a gray shirt underneath his white lab coat.

". . . Have a seat," the doctor said. Like this was an assembly line.

"Just so you know . . ." I took a short breath, standing there. "I'm not Ryodai Kozuka."

". . . Have a seat."

I sat down in a chair. The chair was hard.

". . . So you don't feel like yourself."

I stared blankly at the doctor. This was definitely not okay.

"That's not it . . . just do a DNA test."

". . . DNA test."

The doctor gave me a long look, like I had said something intriguing. I was only stating the obvious, but my words came across as absurd.

"Inside this little hospital of ours," the doctor stated languidly, "we have a large number of patients who won't stop saying they're not sick . . . along with those who say they're someone else."

"But this is different. I'm—"

"The nights are quiet here, but come morning you'll hear them yelling up and down the hall. 'Get me out of here.' 'This is a political conspiracy.' To me, the silence is just the calm before the storm . . . since I know it's coming, even the silence bothers me."

"Come on. I'm not like them."

"In that case . . ."

The doctor stared straight ahead at me.

"Who are you?"

"Huh?"

"I'm asking who you are."

The doctor was still staring at me. It made my head hurt.

"I'm, yeah, I'm . . ."

"Go on."

"*My name is . . .*"

". . . *Stop right there,*" the doctor said.

". . . What?"

"Stop . . . I'm going to be sick."

The doctor winced. This made no sense. The doctor stood.

". . . Let's write you a prescription. Your sense of self . . ."

"That's not what's happening."

"Your sense of self has been divided, creating a separate life."

"No."

This made the doctor smirk. He scratched the corner of his right eye with his pointer finger.

"*I'm well aware you aren't Kozuka.*"

The room felt even quieter than before.

"... What?"

"I was the one who wrote the letter you read in the car. The idea was to get you to come along without resisting, a victim of your own curiosity. Besides, half of it is true ... Come on, there's something that I want to show you."

He led me out into the short hallway, opened the first door on the right and let me in. It was a plain room. A young man, probably in his thirties, sat cross-legged on a chair behind a desk. He looked incredibly serious and dismal, staring off somewhere.

"... Have a look at this."

The doctor took a piece of paper from the pocket of his lab coat and crumpled it into a ball. The dismal man continued staring off somewhere, not so much as a reaction to my entering the room. The doctor tossed the ball of paper on the floor. At first the man did not react, but finally his eyes began to twitch. It looked as if he was exerting effort not to look at the ball of paper. As the twitching grew pronounced, he looked at the paper, averted his eyes, and finally looked at it again. The man stood halfway up, gritting his teeth, and tried to sit back down, but stood up after all. Then he picked up the paper. For a second, he appeared incredibly relieved. Placing the ball of paper on the desk, he began staring off somewhere again, dismal as ever.

". . . That's Kozuka."

". . . Huh?"

My heart sped up.

"He can't stop himself from picking up scraps of paper."

"If you have Kozuka here, what do you want with me?"

"There's something else I want to show you."

The man led me to another room. I swallowed my breath. Something else was rising to the surface.

"What the . . ."

Here's something about me.

Before I went up to that mountain lodge and the man took me to the hospital, I was a doctor of psycho-somatic medicine.

I MAY AS well begin things with the fateful day Yukari first visited my clinic. In keeping with the forecast, a typhoon was approaching, and the air outside was ripe with its arrival, strong winds picking up. Two appointments had been canceled, and she showed up at the deserted office on her own. A tall woman with fair skin. I must have felt the butterflies the first moment I saw her. Confronted by her beauty. She told me she was here because her last clinic closed down, although she had no letter of introduction.

"I can't sleep at night. I have no appetite. I feel like it's happening again . . . maybe because of the typhoon."

I nodded. This squared with the history she filled out before the exam. But I wanted to confirm something with her.

"What medicine were you prescribed?"

"Xanax, Toledomin, Paxil . . ."

She answered without hesitation. A patient familiar with the drugs. Panic disorder and depression. Common enough symptoms.

"When did this begin?"

". . . Is it absolutely necessary that I tell you?"

"To the degree you're able."

"Two years ago . . . after a breakup."

This sounded like a lie. But there was no use forcing the story out of her.

I was not an enthusiastic physician. When I first started out, I used to listen to my patients. But all the things they told me, the stories of their lives, they worked their way inside of me, and at some point I gave up and became a veritable dispensary. Like I had drawn a veil between myself and my patients.

"I'm prescribing you the same medication. A week's worth, for starters."

I noticed her big eyes staring at me. Blinking a few times, on account of her tic. Her eyes were moist.

Maybe I was looking for a reason to quit practicing. At this point it's hard to say.

She stood from her chair and was about to disappear through the doorway, but I told her to wait, unsure of why I stopped her.

"Hold on . . ." I said, scrambling to keep things going. "Have you noticed an improvement from the medication? Something beyond the status quo, an actual improvement?"

A peculiar question. At the very least, not something to ask a patient on their way out the door.

". . . I haven't noticed an improvement. But without the medication . . ."

"Yes?"

"Typhoons . . . terrify me. Because of their size. They make me feel like I've been trapped inside something enormous . . . It gets to the point where I can't leave the house."

". . . When you feel uneasy, take the medicine."

My words felt somehow cold to me. Despite this being what I told everybody else.

THE NEXT TIME she came by, I asked her how the drugs were working. She said they didn't help at all.

". . . Shall I prescribe you something a bit stronger?"

Her eyes blinked, staring back at me.

The rain was coming down outside. I realized she was wearing a short skirt. Though I suppose I must have realized earlier. Shying away, my eyes traveled up her body. When I saw her face, I realized she was smiling. As if to ask if I had caught myself checking out her body. Asking me whether I wanted what I saw.

". . . Doctor."

"Yes."

"I want you to know everything about me."

She stared into my eyes all the more.

"Will you go inside my head?"

". . . Huh?"

"I want to yield myself to you."

"You mean . . ." I avoided looking at her body. "In terms of psychoanalysis?"

She nodded.

I had almost no experience conducting psychoanalysis. Just a little bit in med school. Unlike medication, which takes the edge off, this treatment was a process for awakening the patient to the unconsciously repressed problems inside of them, to the root causes of their ills.

". . . When?"

"Now."

She was my last appointment for the day. Perhaps she had been planning on this all along.

Acting like I had done this countless times, I asked for her to take a seat on the sofa. I walked around the back. Taking a drink from the water cooler, I sorted out what I would do and took a deep breath, careful that she didn't notice.

"You mentioned going through a breakup two years ago . . . Please tell me whatever comes to mind about that time. It's okay to start off with the easy parts."

". . . You mean the facts?"

"No, anything that comes to mind."

I have a tape of what she told me then. In summary, it was something to this effect.

SHE HAD LIKED the man she had been seeing well enough, though she was not especially attached, and the breakup in and of itself had not been very difficult for her. But following their separation, she experienced chronic symptoms of insomnia, loss of appetite and lethargy, and started feeling scared by little things. Places with no exit—moving trains, spaces two or more floors underground—were especially hard to bear. She envisioned herself losing her mind and screaming *let me out*. Sex had been the biggest reason for the breakup. Having sex with him made her feel awful, to the point where just the thought of it drove her to tears.

WHENEVER I ASKED her if she had any sense what was behind it, she grew silent. She said her head hurt, usually adding that it was all a blur. But I caught on to something peculiar. Her memory was fragmentary.

For instance, her memories from elementary school and middle school were extremely vague. She was thirty-two, but drew a blank on various periods of her life. In her own peculiar turn of phrase, they were like holes in the ground filled with plastic.

I became engrossed with her treatment. At that point, I suppose that I had already started liking her. Psychoanalysis is particularly fraught with cases where the psychiatrist and the patient spiral into romance. To give a simplified example, a patient who feels deprived of love from their father may, over the course of treatment, come to see the doctor as a father and attempt to garner love from him. The patient is encouraged to project a variety of important figures from their life onto the doctor. In order to respond, the doctor enters the framework that the patient has established, though working cautiously to keep their distance from the patient. However, like the celebrated analyst Jung—who had sexual relations with a large number of his patients—many fall into the same trap. Was this a romance, or a psychiatric phenomenon common to this sort of case? And supposing it wasn't love, does real love exist? At this point, it's beyond me to say.

I performed hypnosis on her. Once she was in a hypnotic state, I summoned her hidden memories. The practice has fallen out of fashion in the medical community, but Freud often used hypnosis early on. The idea was to bring forth hidden features, making patients conscious they were there, so they could handle them. A way of getting at the root of things.

In her case, things didn't go so well. It's said a quarter of people are particularly receptive to hypnosis, while another quarter are particularly resistant. She was the receptive type. Though very little came up once she had been hypnotized. Sometimes she talked about old TV dramas that it seemed unlikely she had ever seen.

However, one day something peculiar happened.

I had performed hypnosis on her, same as usual. I never swung a watch the way they do in movies. I'd help her relax, sometimes using a mild sedative, and once the workings of her ego had been quelled, I asked her questions. This time she spoke up in a low voice.

"Stop. I'm begging you."

At first, I thought this was her consciousness returning. That she had partially returned to consciousness and was telling me to cut off the hypnosis. But I was wrong.

"No . . . Stop, please stop."

She screamed and tore at her blouse, not dealing with the buttons. The short skirt she had worn that day hiked up her legs. Her breath grew labored.

"Wrong, you're wrong . . . No, I . . . ah, ahh, Doctor Yoshimi."

Yoshimi was the name of the doctor at her previous clinic.

"Stop, ah, no . . ."

Doctor Yoshimi was assaulting her. Strange for this to come up now. She had been a patient of Yoshimi's until fairly recently. It was hard to imagine how she could have managed to unconsciously repress such recent memories so effectively. I tried to bring her out of the hypnosis. But it was no use. She continued to inhabit the person she had been when Yoshimi was assaulting her.

"It's not . . . not what you think," I blurted out.

My thoughts had jumped to the psychoanalysis performed by Pierre Janet.

Janet, like Freud, belonged to the generation of psychoanalysts preceding Jung. He was known for having hypnotized his patients, uncovering repressed events, and successfully replacing them with different memories. As a result, the condition of his patients had improved. Freud and his peers then adopted the practice, though eventually abandoned it. But why? And how come hypnotherapy was no longer utilized in psychoanalysis? The answer is that for the most part, the improvements seen in patients only lasted a short time. The human brain is not something that a doctor can manipulate at will, and the replaced memories will eventually come back. A memory you think you have successfully erased will flap around inside a patient, soon making its way back to where it was.

But I was talking without thinking. Her consciousness was almost fully restored.

"It's not Yoshimi. He never hurt you."

"No, no."

"It's me."

I had no idea what I was saying.

"It's me . . . and I'm not assaulting you."

She groaned, her tone ambiguous.

"I'm holding you gently. In the examination room. And you're raising your voice. Your arms are wrapped around my neck. We're kissing . . ."

Eventually she fell asleep, right there. When she opened her eyes, she stared at me.

"It's like I was dreaming," she said. "That you and I . . ."

I embraced her. She wrapped her arms tightly around my neck, as if to recreate what I had whispered to her under the hypnosis.

BUT AFTER THAT, something even more peculiar happened. The encounter with Yoshimi that I had manipulated through hypnosis disappeared inside of her. I was so sure the repressed memory would eventually resurface and bother her again. There was no way it could have gone so well. I knew I wasn't that good of a hypnotist.

Something else must have been going on. I wound up looking into the whereabouts of Yoshimi, the doctor who had closed his practice.

Yoshimi lived in a Tokyo high rise.

When I visited, he sat down at a round table in a high-back chair and asked for me to take a seat. He received me like I was a patient, as if he had never retired.

I was surprised about how old he was. His closely trimmed white hair was plentiful, but his face was covered with deep wrinkles. Pillar lights stood in all four corners of the spacious room, and an enormous red abstract painting hung on the wall. The expensive carpet was lush underfoot, and the substantial sound-proof windows blocked the passing trains so well they sounded faint and distant.

". . . This is about Yukari."

"Mmh."

Yoshimi was sipping wine. He offered some to me but I declined.

"What did you do to her?"

I wasted no time asking. But Yoshimi showed no sign of agitation. He gave me a puzzled look. As if finding himself with a curious patient.

"Slow down. You look so serious. I'm not following." His voice was hoarse, but strangely easy to make out. "I should be asking you the same thing. What'd you do to her?"

"Performed hypnosis. During which a scene of you and her . . ."

A smile worked its way across Yoshimi's wrinkled face, like he was bristling with delight.

"What's the matter, you jealous?"

"Huh?"

"You're jealous of me. Is that it?"

I looked at Yoshimi with disbelief. But he just kept on smiling. The wrinkles crept up his face.

"That's not all. Her memory is full of holes. What did you do to her?"

". . . Unbelievable." Yoshimi sighed through his smile. "Are you sure you're a psychoanalyst?"

The room was shrouded in the kind of stillness that absorbs sound. I was getting chilly. The air conditioning was on too high. Despite his age, Yoshimi didn't seem to notice.

"Think you can handle her past?"

". . . What?"

"I dunno, maybe you can . . . All right, fine, here's the story."

Yoshimi took a breath. Lips almost closed, breathing in no more than necessary through his teeth.

"She was forced into a sexual relationship with her adoptive father. So she ran away from home, living with a series of men, until she started prostituting herself. Not working under someone else. She went through a series of psychiatrists too. Going back and forth between more stable periods when she could quit the sex work and tougher periods when she had no other choice. When she came to me, she was in crisis. After her fifth failed suicide attempt."

I heard the sound of a train slip into the distance.

"She's severely depressed. In her case, I thought that she might kill herself before I could help her. That's why I did the ECT."

Electroconvulsive therapy. A practice of passing a current through the brain, approved as a treatment for severe depression and other disorders. It had its basis in the observation that patients with epilepsy experienced an improved mood after a seizure, and involved inducing seizure-like symptoms by applying an electric current to the brain, in order to alleviate depression. These days the use of anesthesia made it harmless. Still—

"Understand? Any patches in her memory are a result of that. A classic side effect of ECT. Did that go over your head too? Rest assured, the side effects will go away. Over time, her memory will gradually be restored. Though in her case, the treatment was excessive, so some permanent loss is possible."

"Then why would you do that to Yukari, in her state?"

"Hahahaha."

Yoshimi laughed out loud. His teeth—surely the set he had been born with—were impeccably orderly and trim. Same goes for his peachy gums.

"I guess I was a little jealous of the men who had been with her. Asking myself why those men could have her but not me. I'm an old man. No one wants to sleep with me. So, yeah, that's why."

Yoshimi brought his face closer to mine. His eyelids spasmed.

"You're a psychiatrist, so I'm sure you understand. Into her patchy memory, I hypnotically inserted the fiction of her having sex with me. The spirit of my desire . . . in that sense, I put myself inside of her."

I stared at him aghast.

"You're insane."

"Whoa, whoa. Spare me the free analysis. But say I am. What's so odd about someone my age going insane? So she's having a hard time, huh. *Hahahahaha! That's wonderful. To think I'm sleeping with her, over and over, inside her memory.*"

If I could punch another person, this would have been the time. Instead, I took a deep breath.

"I erased the memory of you."

"Yeah. I'm sure you did. Hypnotically induced memories don't last. Like the memory of dreams . . . Wait a second."

Yoshimi opened his eyes wide. Skinny as he was, his eyes were awfully large.

"You did the same thing too. Didn't you? Used your position as a doctor to initiate a romantic relationship with her. So who are you to show up here and judge me?"

We stared each other down. The room was freezing, but Yoshimi failed to notice.

I was the first to look away.

"I'm going to help Yukari. Her buried memories . . ."

"Whoa, whoa. Take off the rose-colored spectacles. If you draw up every last one of her repressed memories, her life will be impossible to bear. The point is making her forget."

Yoshimi stood up from his chair.

"You're welcome back anytime. To my comfortable abode."

He gave me a faint smile.

"This graveyard of the rich."

BUT THINGS BETWEEN me and Yukari continued peacefully.

Maybe this was one of the stable periods Yoshimi had talked about. Eventually, she was spending all her time at my apartment. She never acted like she disliked having sex with me. We kissed each other softly. She smiled up from under me, gently panting, like it made her feel so happy she was at a loss. As if encompassing me entirely.

Even though it wasn't wintertime, she liked sitting in the heat of the kotatsu. Lots of times she fell asleep there, after eating. Back when we had just met, she had been somewhat provocative, but once we started spending time together, her naivete shone through. When she had fallen asleep in the warmth of the kotatsu, the sight of her face—those eyes which ceased to twitch when she was sleeping—sent a warm feeling through my body, the likes of which I had never experienced before. I tried to wake her up, saying that the sweat would make her catch a cold, but it was no use. She yanked my arm, like she wanted me to snuggle up with her inside the heat, and fell asleep with a smile on her face.

But I began to have misgivings. Did she really care about me? What if my hypnosis was the cause of all of this? Or perhaps this was a transference between patient and doctor, and she never really cared about me after all? Was this different from brainwashing? And if this wasn't love, was there really such a thing?

"Look, I burnt it."

"Let me cook for us," I told her.

"If you throw away the burnt part, there's barely anything left."

"Like I said, let me do the cooking."

Though we were always together, I caught myself stealing glances at her. I had to screw my head on straight. But it was easier said than done. I was unable to stop myself from noticing odd things about her brain, or the structure of the human brain in general. Unable to stop myself from asking what it even meant to be a human being.

"Oh, I burnt this part too. Now there's almost nothing left . . ."

Then she went away.

9

A sandwich had been left unfinished on a plate, but there were no signs of a break-in, and the door had been locked. Her cell phone was off. My heart raced.

I checked her apartment but no one was there. Though I have to say, it hadn't crossed my mind that she'd been caught up in some kind of incident. Maybe I'd expected things to come to this all along. I'd picked up the names of a number of places in the sex industry where she had worked before she started coming to my clinic, as well as where to find the dorms for each establishment. I checked a few without any luck. An image of the terrified face she sometimes showed me out of nowhere appeared before my eyes. I tried another spot, out in the country, taking the Shinkansen. When I arrived, I found her holding bags from the convenience store. This was a dormitory, too, but from the outside it was just another old apartment building. When I saw her she was partway up a narrow flight of stairs.

We met eyes for what felt like a long time. Nothing about her looked surprised. As if she had expected me to have shown up eventually.

"We're hopeless," she said. "This is the sort of place for me. I can't stand the bright lights anymore."

I held her in my arms. She had bandages wrapped messily around her wrists.

Her memory was beginning to come back. Scenes which had never actually been lost, so much as drifted off into the haze, had started taking on a raw vitality, eating away at her spirit once more. The first time her stepfather forced himself upon her. The agony and stink of alcohol. Feeling convinced that she was worthless. Seeing the beautiful city from the window of her room in the sex shop dormitory. How the beauty of the city washed over her. The crowds of men waiting down in the lounge. The harsh body odor of one man in particular. Sleeping with one customer and realizing another man was in the room. How the camera lens closed in. Her mother's suicide. Body stretched and hanging straight down, from the neck. The smell of urine and feces. The malediction her mother left her in her will. Unbelievably, she had not killed herself in an attempt to make amends, but in a drunken stupor, certain that her daughter had stolen her man away. Memories of her actual father. Gaunt and addicted to stimulants. He came to see her after she had started high school. Something clearly abnormal in his eyes, saying this stuff was the real deal, the only drug you'd ever need. "Look at this," he told her giddily. "I love you so much I got a tattoo of your name." The dad who was all talk, who didn't even chip in for their living expenses. Who wore a coat so tattered it was shameful. He had only a few teeth left. The time in middle school he got so high he punched her and her mother six times each.

"Don't worry," I said.

"I'm not worried one bit."

Back at my apartment, I performed hypnosis on her.

"That didn't really happen," I told her, once she was under hypnosis. "You weren't really assaulted by your stepfather. Nothing like that ever happened. Nothing more than a dream, coming from the fear that he might do something like that. In actuality, all your stepfather ever did was lounge around the apartment."

I went on. Not even noticing the passage of the seasons. By her side, every day.

"Your mother didn't commit suicide. Nothing like that ever happened. She wasn't an alcoholic. She was sick in bed. When you went to take care of her, she stroked your head with a frail hand. Gave you a great big hug. Like this. You must remember how that feels? It means she needs you. The world outside needs you too."

By her side.

"Those men never assaulted you. Nothing like that ever, ever happened. You just saw that in a video. At your boyfriend's place. He borrowed the video from a friend, but he was shocked that it was so hardcore. Your old boyfriend wasn't an awful person. He was kind. He may not have had much money, but he saved enough from his part-time job to buy you a present. When he gave it to you, a warm feeling spread inside of you . . . this warm feeling is something that a person feels a number of times in their life. Don't you remember? Come on, he looked like that actor. Why not try imagining his face. His name? What was it—"

Every day.

"You never started a part-time job but had to quit because of being bullied. Nothing like that ever happened. You worked at a café. All the customers who came by loved to see you there. Those customers all had a nice time, thanks to you. You made friends. The friends you met at the café took you to a concert. Don't you remember? The Black jazz artists. You didn't know that much about music, but it made you happy to watch them play, getting into the rhythm. Look, here's the song. This is the song you heard them play. Music is so great. This song will make your bad memories disappear. When you heard it, you caught yourself beginning to sway. You were so moved. By sharing something like this with other people. Immersing yourself in something. You discovered a world you hadn't really known existed. Understand? This world has some wonderful things to offer. Things that can make you come alive inside and bring you joy. Lots of dumb stuff too, but even so, if you look around and really focus on the world around you, there's some pretty good stuff out there too."

It didn't work. Her brain took in the life that I presented her, only to dispose of each piece one by one. I was no Freud or Janet, but even those guys made mistakes all of the time. She disappeared again, until I got a call from a hospital I'd never heard of. She'd cut her wrists. Deep this time. Extremely deep.

When she came home, she clung to me and said, "I want you to do it. That thing Doctor Yoshimi did." Feeling at a loss, I nodded. The device came in the mail. I opened the box.

ECT. I passed a current through her brain. And while her depressive state slightly improved, the memories did not actually disappear as hoped; after a few days she was back to normal. Even giving her a strong prescription—medicine so strong that if you took it you would need to wear a diaper—led to no improvement. "I'm hopeless. I'm never getting better," she said. "I know I'm a burden on you." If I took my eyes off her, she tried to kill herself, and if I tried to stop her she would scream. All that I could do was make her go to sleep.

Aristotle, the scholar from ancient times, supposedly said "Even gods cannot change the past." In which case, the gods are useless. People are different. The past piles up into the present. Some say the past gives us the world we know, or common knowledge, but I reject that view. Why do people need to suffer tragedies? And why do they have to store these tragedies inside their memory, and in so doing, cause themselves pain for the remainder of their lives? If that's a natural fact, then I reject it altogether. Why do we have to suffer like this? Why must we endure such pain? So what if I was faulty in my logic? What did it matter?

"It's okay," I cried, sending the current through her brain. "You were given life. And anybody given life should be able to enjoy it." She was unconscious from the anesthetic. With a shaky hand, I pressed the electrodes to her sleeping head, tears streaming down my cheeks. "What is the past anyway? Who needs it. It may as well disappear. Just a little happiness would do. Enough for you to want to go on living in this world."

I'm not sure if what I was doing qualified as treatment. Perhaps it was, in terms of being a challenge to the structure of the brain. But no. I think that I was pushing back against this thing that we call life. Insisting that people deserved to live in peace. That we could make it through, even when the world was cruel. That a life fraught with misfortune could make the bad stuff disappear.

And even if the gods want for us to live this way, we need not go along with it.

IT WAS A rainy Thursday morning. I wonder what expression I made when I realized her condition, coming off the anesthetic.

Her memories had disappeared. Not only the past, but everything, including me.

You can't just pick and choose the memories you want to disappear. Yoshimi had only managed that by chance and nothing more.

A person can lose their memory by hitting their head, so what would come from this much electricity? If you overdo the ECT, the memory loss can be total. You would have thought I understood that much.

She gave me this long, curious look. Like she was innocently looking at a man she didn't know. Her face incredibly cruel and beautiful to me.

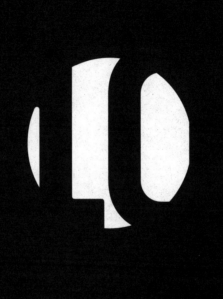

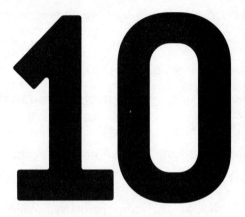

What was I supposed to do now? There was no hope of restoring her memory to normal. Much less working selectively and making her remember only me.

In which case, I thought, there was no choice but to start all over. A brand new life for us.

That night, when I touched her, she took a stance of refusal. But she was gentle, so as not to hurt my feelings. Which made sense. To her, I was a stranger. Intellectually, she recognized that we were dating, but also that I might be lying. As far as she was concerned, I was the doctor who was treating her for memory loss, and nothing more.

When I remembered hypnosis, my heart sped up. I could hypnotize her, directing her to care for me again. But what was the point of getting her back that way? No, I would give up on the hypnosis and work hard to regain her affection.

At the same time, if I labored to regain her affection, and she did begin to show affection toward me, how was that so different from hypnosis? Or from brainwashing for that matter? Was it the difference between conscious and unconscious interaction? Even if I told her our story, working consciously, it would influence the unconscious, feeding back into the conscious in a loop. Which amounts to the same thing. I was losing my conviction. In no time, she expressed that she "wanted to work." I pretended not to notice that these words echoed a desire to escape. She said this to me with her back turned, to help her feign composure. She said the words like it was nothing, but she betrayed her innate awkwardness and didn't sound remotely composed. There was a nice café nearby. The narrow streets around my place were choking with exhaust; this was the only shop that had a slightly foreign air. The café had a sense of freedom, like what you would find on the West Coast of the United States, maybe Los Angeles. About two weeks after she went off to work, she started liking someone. Just like that. She said he liked her too. It was the owner of the shop.

The man came by to meet me. Stopped by, when she was out.

He was a calm guy. Introduced himself as Wakui. Skinny eyes behind his glasses. Chiseled face. His clothes weren't cheap. In a departure from the vibrant mood of the café, he gave me a long, quiet look. Said he was divorced, had been single ever since. No kids from his ex-wife. Managed two other locations under the same name. I was in a daze.

"Things are really complicated," he said. "I mean, we haven't gotten physical or anything like that. I thought that it would be unfair to you."

Yeah right, I thought, but let go of the thought.

Wakui sounded like an honest guy. The right thing was to leave my ugly baggage at the door.

"I've seen the scars she has all over her wrists . . . Could you tell me about her past?"

I wonder what my eyes looked like to him.

My temperature was rising. I heard a mocking crash of sound inside of me, which gave way to a morbid glee that filled me to the brim.

Can you handle the burden of her past? She had a druggie dad and a drunk mom, was sexually assaulted by her stepfather, and found her mom's dead body after she committed suicide. As a sex worker, she fell into a trap and had to sleep with fifteen men at the same time. Seven attempted suicides. Do you realize how many other men have taken pleasure in her body? The inhuman acts of all these men are branded her mind. She only comes across as calm because she's lost her memory. You don't know the real her. Only I do. I'm the only one who can withstand being around her. Because I have a darkness that you lack. Nobody without this kind of darkness is cut out to be her partner. So take your fancy sweater and get out of here.

But I didn't tell him anything. Or couldn't, if I'm

honest. And not out of virtue. I'm not sure what was stopping me.

"I think I more or less have an idea," he told me in a low, steady voice. "I figure she was seriously mistreated by the men in her life. Sexually assaulted and who knows what else, scarred by all kinds of men . . . Am I wrong?"

I wonder what kind of expression I was making. I kept quiet. She was back to zero. She deserved to be happy. It was a surprise to find myself thinking this way. Wasn't it a little late to try to be one of the good guys? Wakui got the message from whatever look was on my face. Like he could see right through me.

He sighed. As deep as any sigh could go.

"Come on . . . I'm fine with all of that."

Dazedly I watched him smile.

"What worried me was maybe she had done somebody harm. Like if she had a criminal record or something. I'm sure that happens now and then, with people who have lost their memory . . . If that were the case, I would want to meet the victim, or the bereaved, and work with her to do our best to make amends. Making up for things together, her and me.

But that would be a difficult situation, tragic for her and everyone involved."

The strength drained from my body. I stared at him for what felt like forever.

"Are you . . . ?"

"Like I said, I own the café."

He smiled. Thin creases at the corners of his eyes. What about his past? Was he carrying around his own personal tragedy? Is that what made him say he could accept her?

"One more thing," he said.

I held a hand up, stopping him from going any further. If he was going to ask, I'd rather say it first.

"You want to know what's going on between me and her, right? Let's just say, we used to be together. But as you know, she doesn't want me anymore . . . So I have no right to hold her back." Was my voice shaking?

He nodded, stood and made his way out of the room. Not wanting to rub it in any more than necessary.

"Please let her know she doesn't need to come here anymore," I said. "She can stay with you, whatever she prefers."

The man nodded again. I had no idea what I would

do if she had come by one last time and looked at me with pity.

I DON'T REMEMBER much of what came next. The carpeting of my apartment soaked up the smell of alcohol. I think I spent a lot of time sitting on park benches. Took satisfaction sitting between those two posts, set into the earth. I never wanted to move again, so I stopped moving. That is, until security came by and made me leave. All I can remember clearly is the time I went by Wakui's café. Seeing her like that, wearing an apron, hair up and smiling as she worked, I nearly collapsed. I had a hard time standing and grabbed the rusted guard rail with my right hand. It took a while for me to notice I was crying.

This was my punishment for trying to change a person's past. My punishment for turning against the gods. I walked up a little farther and vomited on the ground, reminded all too keenly of how much I had loved her. She had appeared out of nowhere and become my everything. This level of affection was a first. For as long as I lived, I knew that I would writhe in agony imagining the humble, peaceful life she and Wakui had discovered, with images of her and Wakui making love assailing me at frequent intervals.

I choked on my own vomit. The pain turned into pleasure and enveloped me. Glad my sorry ass was dying, then and there. Glad to never breathe again. Glad to fall down crying, soaked with puke, be done with it.

11

When I opened my eyes, the white lights drowned my field of vision.

The glare expanded. When I realized I was crying, I saw a man looking me over.

"My memory gets hazy after that. I guess . . ."

"Take it easy," the man said softly. I felt my pulse accelerate. I had only just been at the mountain lodge. With that suitcase.

The suitcase that contained the body of a woman.

"I'm . . ."

"Easy, now," he said. "In your state, this is too much for you. You're all mixed up . . . *Besides, what happened after that was far more terrible than what you've just described.*"

He looked like he was taking pity on me. I didn't care to look him in the eye.

"Let's sleep it off."

The man handed me a pill, which I devoured. It was too much. This reality was way too much for me.

I suppose it was still raining. Hard to say. I tried to distance myself from reality. Knowing I would only wake again.

"Your head is in the clouds. Even if you can pick apart my words, I doubt you can deduce their meaning . . . Isn't that right?"

For a while the man stared into my eyes, then nodded faintly. Things went hazy.

"As far as what came next . . . She committed suicide. The peaceful life that she was living with Wakui was turned upside down. In a flash, her past was back. Two men showed her a video that had been taken of her years before. Their names were Kida and Mamiya."

I heard the voice continue.

"You sought revenge on Kida and Mamiya. Blood-thirsty revenge. Attempting to implant your presence into their conception of reality. Get it . . . Mamiya?"

The man looked like he was smiling, but it was getting hard to tell.

"My name is Wakui. I gave up everything in the name of revenge. And the doctor who's been seeing you all this time . . ."

I faded out.

". . . Get it?"

Dear Wakui:

I figured out where Kida and Mamiya are.

I've also thought up a few ways to get them to the clinic.

Are you absolutely sure you want to get involved with my revenge? I know you've said as much. Considering your feelings, it makes plenty of sense. Like it would be unfair for me to taste revenge all on my own.

I admit I'm torn between wanting to refuse your help, in your best interests, and wanting you to help. Thing is, despite having laid out a plan, when it comes time to make it happen, there's a chance that I might chicken out. Now that I'm this close to getting them, I'm finding myself hesitant because of what comes next. I know these guys did even worse to Yukari. But I think if we go through with it together, I'll be able to acknowledge that we're past the point of no return, and that will help the plan fall into place.

I know I need to change. You must think that I'm pathetic. How can I squander my time like some petty bourgeoisie, now that we've lost Yukari? Who am I to want to kill myself?

I have a few ideas. By the next time we get together, I'll be so different that I come across as a new person. I know this devil of a doctor named Yoshimi. If anyone can change me, it's this guy. Goofy as it sounds for one shrink to go asking another for help.

I want to transcend myself. Becoming something strange, an object that no longer feels warmth, never hesitates to act.

I've attached a file for your reference. For what we are about to do, to some extent it will be necessary for the two of us to share the load.

THERE ARE SEVERAL WAYS TO GET INSIDE
A PERSON'S HEAD. SOMETIMES IT'S SO EASY
IT'S ABSURD, THOUGH AS YOU CAN IMAGINE
THERE ARE TIMES IT DOESN'T GO SO WELL.

Brainwashing has a long history, but "modern
brainwashing" is said to have originated in
Russia. The workings of this system came to light
as the result of an event that took place in 1948
in Hungary, at the time part of the Eastern Bloc.

A theologian was abducted, the secretary of
the cardinal of the Catholic Church in Hungary.
Five weeks later, he returned in the custody of a
police officer.

There was something odd about his eyes,
and while his behavior was suspicious, he was
friendly and relaxed when speaking with the
officer. In short time he led officials to a trap
door in the floor of the basement. When they
opened a golden case that had been hidden in the
earth, they discovered reams of secret documents
penned by the cardinal. Documents that put not

only the cardinal but the entire Catholic Church in Hungary in a predicament. The theologian had been a loyal servant to the cardinal, and anyone would have attested to his character. But now he snickered with delight watching the police seize the cache of documents.

When the cardinal was arrested and appeared before the court, everyone was shocked. This man who was renowned for his high learning and intellect had become another person entirely. His face had changed; rocking incessantly back and forth, he told the court that all that he had ever done was a mistake. Totally confessing to everything, including the preposterous charge of plotting to overthrow the government. He did not appear to be under duress. Rather, he pleaded guilty as if he had lost touch with all emotion.

Most people have heard about the experiments that Russian scientist Pavlov performed on dogs. The main idea was this. If you consistently ring a bell whenever you provide a dog with food, eventually the dog will salivate from the sound of the bell alone. Lenin, the leader of Russia at the time, was deeply moved by this discovery and is said to have declared, "This guarantees the future of the revolution." What most people don't know is there was more to the experiments.

First you ring the bell and give the dog its food. Once the dog gets used to this, it gets confused if you don't give it food. If the dog gets worked up, you give the food as promised. But if you approach the dog calmly and ring the bell nonstop without giving it food, the dog will soon become extremely anxious. Not so much because it wants the food, but from a desperate need for the "predictable, stable sequence" of the bell signaling mealtime. If you then ring the bell and give the food as usual, the dog will become reassured and salivate on cue.

From there, if you immerse the dog in water or otherwise make it feel its life to be in danger, it will completely forget about the "habit" it was forced to learn. Meanwhile, the very personality of the dog will change.

As seen in the Hungarian example, this pattern of conditioning has been applied to human beings in a variety of ways.

First you apprehend a person and confine them. Then you order them to do something like hold their arms up for five hours straight, and when they fail you beat them mercilessly and shower them with abuse. They do their best, resolved to follow orders, but soon discover they'll be beaten and excoriated even if they do. Repeatedly they're asked why they were taken in, and when they voice confusion more violence awaits them. They guess at one thing or another. Eventually they start to mention things they've never done.

This wins them excessive admiration. They feel loved. As a reward, they receive cigarettes or chocolate and are treated kindly. As soon as they feel seen, the verbal abuse resumes without warning. The person desperately attempts to figure out what it is the person interviewing them wants to know. This provokes their survival instincts, and their brain determines whatever thoughts or beliefs they had been carrying to be a casualty, resulting in the brain turning itself inside out. Rather than admitting to a crime supplied by the interrogator, they fixate on a crime of their own making, but since they know their life would be in danger if it's found out to be fake, their brain labels the fabricated crime as the truth. Coercion doesn't enter into it for them, because they confess of their own volition.

This human tendency became a matter of great interest to the United States. Modern brainwashing was thus born in the Eastern Bloc and refined in the West.

Everyone knows about subliminal messaging. In trials at movie theaters, when an image of text saying "popcorn" was spliced into the film, people lined up at the popcorn counter after the show. In other words, instantaneous visual information is able to pass through the consciousness, or "self," and act directly on the unconscious. The unconscious then delivers feedback to the conscious "self," who starts wanting to eat popcorn. The question to which this brings us is perhaps more terrifying than most people think: what, precisely, is the "self"?

There was an experiment known as X-38. Subjects were masked to block their vision and asked to recline in a soundproof capsule, don thick gloves, and place their legs in tubes, so that all their senses would be muted. Out of the twenty-two subjects, half were able to endure a full twenty-four hours. Those who did suffered from disorientation, a jumbled sense of distance, impaired ability to think or concentrate, auditory and visual hallucinations, and feelings of paranoia.

Why? Because the brain requires a moderate amount of "information." An excess of information will cause disturbance in the brain as well, but when information is seriously lacking, the brain is unable to perform its usual functions and greedily desires stimuli. If you play a tape expounding an idea or opinion in the capsule, these starving brains will find it irresistible. The content will bypass whatever the self is thinking, and the unconscious, or the recesses of the mind, will latch onto it ravenously. The result was that the content of the tape had a huge influence on the personalities of those who heard it, even after they had left the capsule.

There have been numerous incidents where people were manipulated in such a manner. Take this example from Denmark in 1951. A man arrested for bank robbery was discovered to have been brainwashed into committing the crime. He was also brainwashed into marrying a woman and subsequently handing his wife over to the brainwasher.

When attempts were made to free him from hypnosis, the man vehemently resisted, as he had been hypnotized into fighting back should a person come along and try. To snap him out of it, they used the primitive method of flooding his system with tranquilizers as soon as he became recalcitrant. The trance was broken, but he was so "hypnotically susceptible" that mention of the letter "P" would put him back into a trance.

Incidentally, adherents of the cult group Aum Shinrikyo, who released the lethal sarin on Japanese subways in 1995, killing or injuring a large number of people, are said to have had these words hypnotically embedded in their minds:

"If someone tries to wake you up, self-destruct."

Such tactics have obviously been adapted for use by the military and intelligence communities. A person is hypnotized and given top-secret information, only to be recollected when a specific person utters the phrase chosen as the password. Meanwhile, the person forgets they were ever hypnotized. This was all within the realm of possibility. As was forcing prisoners of war to confess. It's been discovered that those under hypnosis have an astonishing command of their memory. Even incredibly long passages of secret information can be retained if communicated under hypnosis.

Drugs offer another way of causing direct changes in people and have changed history in their own right. Hitler is widely known to have taken massive doses of drugs like methamphetamine (known in Japan as Philopon or speed). The drug has various side effects, delusions of persecution among them. How many were persecuted because of Hitler's paranoia? Sufficient attention has not yet been given to the role played by his attending physician, Theodor Morell, who doled out his steady stream of medication. A variety of evidence exists that methamphetamines were taken by the kamikaze pilots of the Japanese Special Attack Units, just before taking off. Today, radicalized soldiers and terrorists are given all kinds of illegal drugs. As a result, they are able to do things they otherwise could never do.

From here, the history of brainwashing enters an extreme stage with ECT, originally a treatment for depression. A direct current of 100 volts is applied to induce seizures. The idea comes from how people living with epilepsy show a temporary boost in mood after a seizure. These days patients are given anesthetic beforehand. Muscle relaxants are used in what is called non-electroconvulsive therapy.

Occasionally misused for torture, these devices are advantageous because low voltages do not result in external injuries. ECT can have the side effect of memory loss. By using low voltages for torture and finishing off with a dose high enough to cause a seizure, it is possible to make the victim forget that they were ever tortured.

If a person injures the hippocampus area of the brain, they can become unable to form new memories, but old memories will remain intact.

These "long-term memories" are said to be stored in the cerebral cortex, which is the same portion of the brain affected by ECT.

Cases have been documented where excessive ECT has caused a total loss of memory, as well as cases of entering a childlike state. Ordinarily, the memory will be restored over time, but there are cases where it has been lost for good.

If an onslaught of statements and opinions is directed at a person in this "childlike state," they will be absorbed by the "clean slate" of their brain. This means that if you tell them "you like being kind to others," they will assume a benevolent attitude. If you tell them "you can't resist picking up scraps of paper," the patient will be that way forever.

This outcome is absolute.

What is a "self"? Under a particular set of circumstances, it becomes impossible to tell.

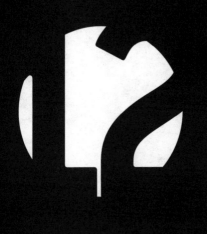

The doctor called me into his office. There was something familiar about this doctor. I couldn't simply
overlook it.

"How are you feeling?" he asked. When I came in
he was in the middle of writing something, but he set
about turning off the screen to his PC.

"Not too bad. Except . . ."

"Except what?"

"One section of my memory feels out of sync."

I was telling the truth. As painful as it was to disappoint the doctor.

"I know I lost my memory, and that you and the other doctors are trying to help me get it back. Pointing things out, so I can see them for myself. These memories feel familiar, but I dunno, like something from a dream, and won't gel with the memories that really feel like mine. There's a disconnect. Either it's me, or it's my memory . . ."

The doctor frowned. It made me want to please him. These people were the only hope I had. I'd lost touch with who I was. It felt like the trees were coming through the windows. I was swarmed with terror. I took a deep breath, trying to calm down, but it was no use.

"Okay, but remember yesterday, when you were telling me about your memories, how eloquently you described everything with Yukari? Well . . . you were reading from an old journal of yours. From the way you read the passages aloud, without one hiccup, it sounded like the person in the journal was the you here in the room, telling his story. You told me all about how Yukari went off with a guy named Wakui, so emotionally invested you broke down in tears."

"Yeah. The more I read, the more familiar it all felt to me."

I glanced outside the window. There they were. Too many trees to count.

". . . Hold on to what resonated with you. The self inside your memory. Over time, you'll come to recognize him as a part of who you are . . . How much do you hate the men who hurt Yukari?"

"So much."

The doctor looked like he was smiling, all too pleased to hear me say this. I must have been seeing things. My head was pounding. Worse than yesterday.

"When I think about how much I hate them, it makes those memories feel even more like a part of me."

"Stay with that."

"Okay."

I looked away from the trees outside the window, but my heart was pounding.

"Sleep it off. Lots more therapy to come."

[Unprinted file]

After discovering the whereabouts of Mamiya
and Kida, I paid a visit to Yoshimi. Same high-
rise apartment as before. Again he welcomed
me as if I was a patient. I sat down in the chair
across from him.

". . . Yukari committed suicide."

When I told him this, Yoshimi showed no

sign of agitation. Nothing but a subtle twisting of his wrinkled lips.

"Really."

"Doesn't that make you sad? What with you and Yukari."

"I'll be dying soon." Yoshimi sounded oddly enthused. "The more company I have the merrier."

He looked all too pleased. I gave him a blank stare. Of course, I thought. What else would I expect from him. Feelings of resignation and envy flattened the power I had felt inside of me.

"So, what of it? Thinking of killing yourself and hoping I can set you straight? That much I can do, I suppose."

"That's not it."

Through the window, the sound of a train slipped into the distance. As if taking something away from me.

"I want for you to change me. Into a scumbag like you."

Yoshimi smiled.

"You want revenge?"

"Yeah."

"Marvelous . . . Good for you."

His response did not compute.

". . . What are you saying?"

"Have you honestly forgotten?"

Nothing could be heard outside the window.

"The first time you and I met."

My pulse was getting quicker by degrees.

". . . Huh?"

"After you injured your mother, they sent you to reform school, what we now call a home for troubled youth. I was the doctor who fixed your head."

The memory was far from lucid, but I did recall several different doctors taking turns examining me. Come to think of it, he did remind me of one of them. But that doctor had had a large build. It didn't add up. Though I suppose if he had lost a lot of weight and aged . . .

"You were an interesting kid. Some creepy territory in that little head of yours, but you didn't seem to notice. Or maybe, those creepy parts of you never entered your juvenile consciousness.

Taking on some other peculiar form to exercise their ill intent . . . This was over twenty years ago. I've aged a lot since then. It's hard for me to say . . . Ryodai Kozuka."

". . . Excuse me?"

"I knew this guy, another doctor like me, without any kids. I'm the one who recommended that he and his wife take you in . . . You had an interesting history, and they seemed up for the task of raising you. Besides, you were a bright kid, so there was the possibility that you could take over the family practice someday."

Yoshimi raised the wine to his lips. Until then, I hadn't noticed he was drinking any.

"That was years ago. I've basically forgotten. But when that doctor passed away, and I showed up at the funeral to pay my respects to this thoroughly ordinary man, the new father who raised you, I got word that you had taken over his little practice. I'm the one who told Yukari to head over and see you. Know why?"

I had a hard time putting it all together. His words weren't getting through to me.

"Never mind, I've gone too far already
. . . Let's talk about me for a sec."

Yoshimi worked his wrinkly little mouth, like
he was chewing something.

"I'll skip the details of my upbringing. But
dark as things were for me, I turned out okay.
Not a massive success, but not a massive failure.
As a psychiatrist, I never slacked off, though I
was never especially motivated either. A quiet
life, no friends, but if someone approached me
I responded personably enough. That's the kind
of man I was."

He nodded at his own declaration.

"I saw a great number of patients. Ten years
passed, then twenty. Every one of them hurt in
a different place, minds wounded in a different
way. I did my best to heal them. In a generic
way, indifferently. Sometimes things went well,
and other times, they didn't. One day, this kid
showed up. Late twenties, unemployed. Here's
what he says: I think I may have killed someone
. . . Follow? Fear of inflicting harm, an aspect
of obsessive-compulsive disorder. I asked him

when. He said just now. He was in a tight spot all right. Terrified that he might kill someone, or perhaps already had. A vague suspicion he had killed someone without so much as realizing, on the street, or at the store, like he could feel it in his hands, like maybe at the railroad crossing, sure, down at the railroad, when that old person was in front of him, he must have pushed them down onto the tracks . . . Every line of thought was painful, tinged with a fear that he would be arrested. He quit leaving the house, so that he could record his every move. That way, if he started worrying he might have killed someone, he would have a record he could turn to and see otherwise . . . Situations vary, but with this particular patient, my sense is there was somebody he hated, who he wanted to kill, and that his feelings of guilt about wanting to kill them had resulted in these symptoms . . . The day he came, I wasn't feeling very well. I probably should have taken the day off, but my work ethic was the one serious thing about me. On my way down to the exam room, I could have sworn I saw this tiny middle-aged woman, a patient of mine, hiding in the shadows of the cardboard boxes piled in the hallway. She said she had a secret, whispering in a conspiratorial sort of way. She breathed on her fingers, like they were freezing, then scratched her face and let me have the secret, which involved some trivial rumors about a family in the neighborhood. With this grave look on her face . . . I shrugged off the vision right away, but recognized I really should have taken the day off. I knew I had to set this patient straight, prescribe behavioral therapy, tell him the drug options . . . but for whatever reason I just sat there in a daze, listening to him talk."

Yoshimi's eyes went vacant for a second, before snapping back to normal.

"I knew I had to do something about this patient, or else there would be trouble, but I was consumed by an overwhelming lethargy and let it all go in one ear and out the other. As if none of it really mattered. Who cares. What difference did it make who this guy killed,

whose life he ruined? I should have been horrified at myself for thinking such a thing. But
the lethargy was so profound I didn't have the
energy to spare. The only thing in proper order
was the tick-tock of my heart. Until I came out
with it."

". . . Came out with what?"

"That maybe he had already done it."

The air conditioning hummed away.

". . . The guy was shocked. He must have
thought I'd tell him that I knew he didn't do
it, whereupon he would assure me he was
pretty sure he had . . . but contrary to his
expectations, I proposed that he had probably
killed someone before he started keeping the
journal. I told him I'd seen countless patients
who had done the same thing. Start a journal,
just like him, only to find out they had killed
somebody long before. Obviously I was lying.
But I said it anyway. All the while telling myself
it was wrong, that I had to take it back . . . he
was thoroughly stunned, but I prescribed a
gentle headache medication and sent him

on his way, knowing that I really should have written him a proper script."

Curling his lips, Yoshimi smiled again.

"Later on, I caught a bit of news. A slasher in a crowded street. Several dead and many wounded. The offender was an unemployed guy in his twenties . . . When I saw that on the news, it brought me to a place beyond good and evil. It was beautiful. Persecuted by society, he had bottled up this hatred, but now that hatred had been paid back with interest. The victims caught the backlash, their lives made into vectors, spreading it even farther. What I was watching were the lines. Black strings. In my eyes, this was not about good or evil, but a scientific phenomenon, like in physics, when elementary particles influence each other and give rise to some kind of an event. Watching those black lines scatter, I thought their flowing motion was so beautiful."

Yoshimi drew a quick breath.

"You told me about those strings. But at the time I did my best to calm you down, honest man I was. But now the time has come for you to call upon the powers that you had when you were young."

The room was cooling down.

"If I'm able to restore them, you may be cut off from your life as you know it. Your favorite things, like drinking coffee at cafés, or music, or remembering the first time that you saw the city, things like that may no longer give you the warm sensations that they did before, once the cold blood is coursing through your veins. This is the tradeoff for passing over to the other side. To make a dream come true, something must be sacrificed."

My heartbeat was audible, like it was fighting back. I grinned.

"Fine by me."

I pressed the record button on the digital recorder in my pocket, curious to hear his approach.

[(From Recording) (Unprinted File)]

—Human beings are innately aggressive.

Yoshimi's voice.

—Freud contended this arises from the
force that returns all living things
to inorganic matter. As if rewinding

things, back to the basic elements of
physics. He also drew comparisons to
the forces of attraction and repul-
sion . . . which makes a lot of sense.
But I'm more interested in considering
this innate drive in terms of human
beings and life in general.

*A scraping sound. Moving in my seat, I must have pushed
the mic against the fabric of my pocket.*

—Needless to say, living things must
feed on one another to survive. Our
innate aggression is a natural and
essential tool for maintaining our
existence. That said, human beings
no longer hunt, with limited excep-
tions. Our aggressive impulses are left
hanging . . . leading us to exercise our
impulses by altering their form and sub-
stance. Sex is part of this. Penetration,
as an act, requires aggression. I tend
to think that this applies on a greater

scale as well, both to the tendency of
men to blame others and that of women to
blame themselves . . . Never mind, that's
garbage.

*Yoshimi laughed. I'm sure that I was still awake, but I did
not respond.*

—Thus our innate aggressiveness, let's
call it evil, finds a way to spread.
When we examine this human drive, it's
impossible to draw a line between what
constitutes aggressive behavior and
what does not, since aggression can
all too easily be sublimated into other
forms. Channeled into wholesome things
like fascination with a certain topic
or complaining about life at the bar,
which on first glance have nothing to
do with our aggressive impulses. But
oftentimes we tap into this energy
directly. We may turn this aggression
inward, for example, giving ourselves a

hard time. That's how it was for Yukari.
Although she was the victim, she blamed
herself and continuously hurt herself as
well. All of this pent-up aggression
causes people to internalize those
who have harmed them, so that they
inflict harm on themselves as a way of
exacting their revenge . . . You have
that tendency yourself . . . Though
in the case of actual criminals
. . . let's see, who would be a good
example?

"How about Tsutomu Miyazaki?"

—Why him?

"I've done some research on him. To
discover how someone so apathetic
could do a thing like that. I've also
looked into Hiroshi Maeue. The guy
who killed three people he met on a
suicide site . . ."

—Hoping to find the intrinsic factor
for their crimes, so you can transcend
your personal limitations?

"Yeah. Miyazaki did that by
surrendering himself to the Rat Men—"

*At this point, my memory began to blur. The medicine
was working.*

—Tsutomu Miyazaki was beaten up in
school right? And I bet the guys who
bullied him are out there living happy
lives. The evil multiplying in their
hearts. Despite being completely unin-
volved, the people who hurt Miyazaki are
connected with the little girls Miyazaki
murdered. At least, in the convoluted
workings of Miyazaki's brain. The world
as we perceive it can be viewed as a
network of vectors. Packets of evil
spreading through the network. Take a
certain commentator from the newspaper.

Adamant about the need for war and the
superiority of Japanese people. But once
upon a time, he was my patient. A puny
guy with no self-confidence, who rein-
vented himself by aligning his identity
with a robust nationalism. An archetypal
pattern in psychoanalysis. It's said
that those who engage in hate speech
will experience a boost in health the
following day. Most people live their
lives ignorant of who they really are.
The more scared a person is, the less
likely they are to delve into the
question. Needless to say, war presents
an opportunity for the aggression of
large numbers of people to be exercised
vicariously, though in reality, providing
no more than a shell of goodness to
crawl into.

Yoshimi laughed. Alone.

—Take a look around the internet. The

ditches into which all evil is eventually swept. People hide their faces
and type away without a care, no self-
awareness for how their words will be
picked up by others, forming a chain.
When human beings can cover their
faces and hide behind a shield of
goodness, they release their aggression without hesitation. Not even
realizing their aggressiveness for
what it is. This has to end, if not
today then soon . . . Anyway.

Rustle of clothing.

—Seems like the meds are working. I
doubt you'll garner anything of use
from looking into Tsutomu Miyazaki.
In my view, he didn't have dissociative identity disorder, but
something lighter, schizophrenia.
With schizophrenia, you can become
convinced you're someone else, that

everything around you is an enemy,
and can even claim that you're a god.
Symptoms vary, but having a dictator
appear inside your head is one of
them. That's what's going on when a
criminal says the voices made them do
it. In my estimation, there was probably also some premature sexualized
play between him and the guy with the
emotional disorder who looked after him
. . . I think we can agree that there
are different, better models we can
follow. Granted there's some overlap,
but it's not like I can pick you up
and drop you down inside a complicated
illness . . . I know you're thinking
about suicide. However, there's a possibility of that urge being no more
than innate aggression flaring up and
turning inward. You're feeling guilty
about Yukari. That makes you want
to punish yourself. There's even a
feeling that your death would amount

to revenge on the wider world. Better
nip that in the bud.

I gave no response.

—I still have your chart from way back
when I examined you. Let's return there
for a spell. Just after something made
you push your mother, and she gave you
that tempting look. You were trying to
align yourself with the men who beat
your mother, but then you rejected the
idea. Isn't that right?

No response, but I must have nodded.

—Thought so. This time, I want for you
to go full circle, really becoming the
men who beat you and your mom. Follow
their lead . . . The world is teeming
with unhappiness. It's scary out
there. Horrifying. But why be crushed
by that unhappiness, when you could

take position at the root, where it's
created? On the side making the world
unhappy.

"You want me to be like those guys?"

My voice, but it sounded like a little kid.

—In this case, you have no choice but
to exploit the evil you know best.
Last time, you fell short of being a
real criminal.

"But I'm . . ."

—You said you wanted to give up your
identity. Guess what? That's what happens
when you open yourself up to evil.

Rustling clothing.

—Besides, these are the guys who hurt
Yukari. Anything goes.

"But that takes guts . . ."

—Correct. Which you don't have.
That's why something deep inside of
you took over, when you pushed your
sister and injured your mom. And how
come you lack guts? Because you're
still trying to ally yourself with
the world. Because you don't want to
be cast off by society. Time to flush
that down the drain. You're better
off turning your back on the world.
Try to conjure up that feeling. The
pleasure you felt after pushing your
sister. After knocking down your mom.

"But afterward . . ."

—Nope. Focus on the circumstances.
Exclusively on what was going on.

*This time the rustling sound lasted a while. It seemed like
I was fidgeting a great deal.*

—It felt great. Am I right? And this
time, you'll do it of your own accord.
Taking down Kida and Mamiya. Those
guys who called Yukari out at the
café. It's going to feel great.

"Not like it matters. I want to die."

—Turn that self-hate on your enemies.
Don't change it into something else.
Trade your good health for revenge.

THIS SORT OF *dialogue continued. For hours. Some-*
times I nodded off, just barely coming to, and nodded off
again. Until the battery on the recorder died.

—You're leaving this world. Heading someplace far beyond the clustered lights. A
place that's incredibly cold. Your blood
will run ice-cold in your veins.

[Unprinted File]

Stringing along Mamiya and Kida was a cinch. I hired someone to look them up. Mamiya grew up pretty close to me, and Kida used to work in a factory that was close to my apartment. Faced with the heady events about to unfold, I felt a peculiar awareness of cause and effect.

They didn't know that Yukari had killed

herself. These guys were customers from back when she worked at the sex shop. They had shown up out of nowhere, pressuring her to sleep with them for free using a sex tape from her past as blackmail.

It was Kida who first saw Yukari working at Wakui's café. Lusty at the sight of her, he tried to say hello; but by then she had forgotten everything. Kida thought that she was messing with him, so he burnt the video onto a DVD and dropped it off, warning her that she would have to sleep with them again, or else they'd put it on the internet.

She should have asked Wakui what to do. I wish she had. But once the memories were back, she hanged herself impulsively. Same as her mother. A suicide note was left beside the DVD, written in a crazed hand.

Now I remember everything. No more.

Her dark side, subdued and looking for a way out, must have seen an opportunity in the relapse of her memory. Raiding her senses, this transient force told her to end her life, like it was now or never. Quick, while Wakui was away. As if a hole had been torn open in the fabric of time, and she had let herself fall through.

Wakui was gaunt and stunned, but I was unable to form a sentence, much less console him. I'd gone over the edge. He had given me the news over the telephone. I basically can't remember. I think I spat out something incoherent. I was at home. Feeling myself plummeting, I stumbled over to the wall and slumped down to the floor. Water fell in droplets from the sink, asserting its existence, individual drops at even intervals. Only ever moving one direction, plinking drop by drop. A natural law. A desolate fact. This tepid, frank display was absolutely terrifying.

He came by. I could have sworn that I had gotten up, but I was still leaning against the wall. Wakui took a seat somewhere. Feels like we sat like that for hours. Like a bizarre set of twins. Wakui finally said, "Let's kill those guys." To which I nodded.

Earlier, I wrote about my visit with Yoshimi.

Reason I did was I wanted to die. Sure I wanted revenge. I couldn't let them get away with this. But my own will to live had become perilously thin.

I had hoped that after seeking his advice, an evil force would occupy my body, but instead I became exceedingly collected. My death wish became less pronounced. I essentially lost interest in dying. Even the idea of killing those guys had begun to lose its charm. What I had in mind was something far more crucial than all that.

When someone dies, we tell whoever is to blame to think of how the bereaved family must feel. We also sometimes tell them they deserve a taste of their own medicine. This idea agreed with me. I wanted to inject them with my very being. Destroy whatever life they had created and replace it with my own, a full transfusion of its darkness. They would turn into me, experiencing for themselves the nightmares I experienced. Let the nightmares compact their minds.

Wakui was on board with my proposal. He had one condition: "After that, we're gonna kill them." I said that I was on board with that plan too.

So I made contact with Kida and Mamiya. I had chickened out the first time, unable to go through with it, but this time I went up to them like it was nothing. "Hey, I'm Yukari's husband," I said. "I saw the video. Great stuff. Could you do that with her again for me, in the same way? I want to watch you do it. I'm ready to pay. How's two hundred thousand yen sound?"

I played the kinky husband smitten with his wife. They grinned and laughed. Buy us a drink, they said, so I bought them drinks. Don't worry, they said, we'll take real good care of your wife. Get this. When you do this to her, know what she does? Or how about when you do this? Strange how casually I listened to them talk and let them wrap their arms around my shoulders. I guess I was no longer my old self. That self was working its way into them.

I asked for them to do it at the clinic. When

they came by I met them at the door. Drugging their coffee didn't make me feel the least bit nervous. It was easy.

Wakui and I looked down on them. Out cold all right. To make them easier to move around, we moved their bodies onto gurneys and strapped them down. Ordinarily you give a patient anesthetics and muscle relaxant before doing ECT. But not this time. We worked swiftly, without hesitation. Upon sending a low current through their brains, they blurted nonsense and opened their eyes.

The brain defines the terms of our existence; and the ability of electricity to influence these terms cannot be fathomed. Lashed securely to the stretchers, their bodies spasmed violently under the current. It must have sounded like we were enjoying ourselves. But Wakui and I were expressionless, letting it run. Listening to them plead and beg forgiveness, I thought about how ugly they were. Faces wet with tears and snot, foam dripping from their mouths. ECT without anesthesia, liable to fry their brains. For starters, I cranked Kida's current up from low to high. He passed out; and when he came to, he was spaced out like a toddler. Not a word. I mixed up a strong medication and fed him a heavy dose. He no longer had a need for the basic premises of his existence, of being who he was.

"Your memory is hazy. So let me tell you who you really are."

I made him read the notes that I had started writing. To make Kida into a second me, another Kozuka. "Turn this page, and you may give up your entire life." When I had written that first line, I felt a sense of glee. To change myself, I had done research on real criminals—Tsutomu Miyazaki, Hiroshi Maeue—so I added those analytical passages to the packet. All the ups and downs since losing Yukari, the trials I had undergone to transform and steep myself in evil, so that I could take revenge—the entire contents of my head would soon take over their existences. You may be wondering why I chose Miyazaki and Maeue, out of all the criminals in the world. I had my reasons, but I'll save that for another time.

Kida continued reading, with the obedience of a young child. If he stopped, I punished him. I was using operant conditioning, the kind practiced once upon a time in psychiatric hospitals in America. Problematic patients were strapped down, and if they misbehaved they hit them with enough electricity it hurt. Before the zap, they rang a buzzer, so that over time the sound of just the buzzer made the patients listen up. Who knows how many times I flipped the switch on Kida, or how many times I rang the buzzer. Shut off in his own room, he continued reading my notes. Soon he became convinced that this was him and started begging me to stop. When I asked him what to stop, if he was really who he thought he was, he cried and told me just to stop already. He needed more. I hypnotized him countless times. Finally, he started crying as he read the pages. He was starting to become emotionally invested.

But things did not continue going well.

Before long, he became resistant. Whether I rang the buzzer or switched on the electrodes made no use, because he had stopped acting like an invalid. It was a bust. I would have to start all over. I did another round of ECT, even stronger than before. Fine by me if his brains burnt to a crisp. So I dramatically increased the dose of medication. Once I embedded the idea that he was unable to resist picking up scraps of paper, he was soon able to do that much just fine—but unable to do anything else. He was no longer human, but some other kind of bizarre creation.

In an attempt to turn Kida into another me, I had damaged his brain beyond repair. I would need to handle Mamiya more carefully.

Rather than forcing him to read about Kozuka's life, meaning my life, I painstakingly hypnotized him into thinking that his name was Kozuka, and that he had a certain type of personality. Really taking my time. But he wound up a bizarre creation too. As I continued to administer strong doses of medication, he began to lose his memory in pieces, which led to schizophrenia. The human brain is complicated. Mamiya began to claim he had acquired Kozuka's identity. Perhaps his brain had recoded the repetitive messages into a memory of a voluntary act. Those with schizophrenia become convinced they're being badmouthed by their neighbors, or frightened by implausible things they overhear, or think they're someone else. Far from an exception, Mamiya was fixated on the idea that he had taken on a new identity and had to run away, as if he was the central character in some epic adventure. If I could reinforce that train of thought, before long I would occupy him totally. Or so I thought.

However, exploiting his morbid fixation on having taken on a new identity would not give us enough leverage to make him think he was Kozuka. Somewhere along the line, we would need to make him suspect that he had not actually changed his identity, but had been Kozuka all along. As I would have had to when treating such an ailment, I was forced to sail into treacherous seas, often losing my way. I had to make him feel uneasy, while perpetuating his condition. My thought was that perhaps I could rewire his brain by placing him in adverse circumstances and conditioning him to think that a complete transformation into Kozuka would save his life. Like the experiments they used to do in Russia. To get things going, I co-opted his fixation by delivering him to the rundown mountain lodge that I inherited from my father—the doctor who had taken care of me after the children's home. The plan was to alter his surroundings, thus setting him on edge, and finally have him read through my account.

Before sending him off to the lodge, Wakui had caught Kida, after his nervous breakdown, scribbling into the pages of the account, in that slanted script that was so obviously his. Wakui urged me to erase them, but I preferred to let them stay. Seeing those scribbles would surely crank up Mamiya's anxiety, a condition I believed I could exploit in order to compromise the seat of his beliefs. Somehow, he thought the doll inside the suitcase was an actual dead body. Apparently he shut the lights off when he heard Wakui ring the bell, but did he really think that doll was real? The doll that I had ordered in the likeness of Yukari, to help me stay alive. I found a doll maker who took on this kind of thing. He was a kind man with pale skin and long hair. I placed my report on Hiroshi Maeue inside the suitcase too, but apparently Mamiya never read it.

I sent Wakui up to check on him, but things were going rather poorly. Wakui was unfazed, albeit somewhat pushy, and reassured him several times that he was in fact Kozuka. I had sent him off with a letter that I wrote to put his mind at ease. In the space of a few sentences, I used the word "relax" twice. When toying with a person's mind, you need to inspire a mixture of danger and safety. Especially the sort of danger that pops up when you're feeling safe. Despite my best attempts, however, to emulate all manner of classic brainwashing techniques, I was unable to pull it off. In principle it should have worked, but in practice it was all fouled up. Things had not gone as planned.

It seemed that he was verging on remembering his name, though he had failed to recognize the man we told him was Kozuka was in actuality his buddy Kida. Oh well, I thought. Though acknowledging that I might fry his brains completely, I decided to subject him to excessive ECT, like Kida. When I said "there's something else I want to show you" and showed him the device, he finally looked surprised. Or perhaps seeing the device made him remember everything that had been done to him.

I then subjected Mamiya to several rounds of high-voltage ECT. The next day, when I observed him after he came to, it made me gasp. He had not simply forgotten things. His memory loss was almost total. Same as Yukari.

While he remained fixated on some recent images, like having visited the mountain lodge and seen the body of a woman in a suitcase, things like his name had been expunged from his memory. Through hypnosis, I continued to whisper to him that his name was Kozuka, meaning he was me. Day after day, week after week, I addressed his unconscious. He absorbed what I said to a frightening degree. Now that it was empty, his brain devoured information ravenously. He even made it to the point where he could trust us. As if we were actually a kindhearted doctor and his aide, committed to restoring his memory. On top of that, while reading through the manuscript, he gradually began to utter hateful things about Kida and Mamiya. I almost cracked up, in spite of myself. Watching this guy say those things, no idea that he was Mamiya. I knew I had to proceed with the utmost caution. Having come this far, there was no time to waste.

I came up with a way of using Kida in his vacant state. Mamiya would be next. Our revenge would soon come to fruition.

Simple lines are far more beautiful than lines that shoot off randomly. Who cares about a slasher? I would take the black string from inside of me and plant it in their heads unadulterated.

I stared up at the lights in the ceiling. Lately, it felt like this was all I ever did.

A photograph was on the desk. A photo of Yukari. When I looked at the photo, it registered that I was in love with her. She had the sort of face I like. That probably sounds pretty weird. I mean, Yukari and I used to date. But then she went away. She killed herself.

Tears ran down my face. It was almost like the two of us had actually dated. But wait, we really had. It was just taking me a long time to warm up to this reality and to admit that it was mine.

When I tried remembering what happened in the past, it made my head hurt. Which would be all right on its own, but I dunno, it made me anxious. All the same, when I thought about my sister who fell off the cliff, or my mother who drank, for some reason it made me feel relieved. You would think these memories would be unpleasant. I looked at old photos of them. I had looked over these photos countless times. What was my sister up to? Did she resent me? The door opened. It was the doctor.

"Doctor," I said, "I need my medicine. My heart is pounding. I feel uneasy."

"I just gave you some, remember? You took it a few minutes ago."

"The drugs aren't working. Something else is going on."

"Really . . ." The doctor almost looked like he was smiling. "How are you feeling?"

"Like I told you, not so good . . . besides." I told the doctor something that had been bugging me for quite a while. "Maybe it's because I'm feeling crazy . . . but I dunno . . . I'm starting to feel like Yukari died because of the treatment I gave her."

The doctor looked at me directly.

"Say more."

"I'm not sure what else to say." I took a deep breath. Last thing I wanted was to start crying midsentence. I had turned into such a crybaby. "I just have a feeling . . . but it's not like I can draw a line between myself and what happened . . . just sort of a question . . . did I really hypnotize Yukari and give her ECT, trying to make things better? . . . Plus the revenge thing."

"Revenge?"

"Against my mother," I said. "I think that what I really wanted was to fix her. Hard to make sense of it now . . . but that feels true. Maybe it has to do with how I'm still talking about myself like I was someone else . . . but without me even realizing, my resentment toward my mother must have carried over to Yukari . . . though maybe none of this makes sense."

"You mean you noticed that too?"

". . . Huh?"

"I was thinking the same thing. Like maybe you pushed her—Yukari—over the edge."

[Unprinted File]

This must have happened before I pushed my sister off the cliff. A single, blurry memory.

I was coming home from school, partway up the hill. Suddenly I froze, unable to go any farther. Because the house was high above the town, I had to keep on going up, but I felt this sinking feeling of fatigue throughout my body that prevented me from going any farther. It was like my body was refusing. Why do I have to climb a hill like this to go back to a house like that? Climbing the hill meant returning to my life, once I had made it to the top.

The house was in view. The lights were on. The car was parked outside, so for some reason Dad must have been home. The usual oppressive dinner would be starting soon. My grouchy dad, unrelated by blood, my frightened mother, my grandma, always worrying about my sister, and my sister, who acted happy trying not to face the facts. This was who I had to sit with at the dinner table.

My thoughts went to a particular episode. One day, when I was feeling lonely, I had used one of my sister's tricks and complained that I didn't want to eat my dinner. Dad glared at me. Damn, I thought. I realized I was acting out of line. I would need to pay renewed attention to my every action and only do the things I was supposed to be doing. I had to cast aside my loneliness and any other wretched feelings I might have. Or so I told myself, though casting them aside had proven to be impossible.

As I was looking up the hill, the sky above the house had started getting dark, accentuating the light coming from the windows. Why bother with the lights in a house like this? From where I stood, I watched the silhouettes of the other four members of the household through the windows. Since I doubt that I could actually see them, I suspect that this was something I imagined at the time, which later made its way into my memory and became a part of my past. I was the anomaly. Without me, the family would be whole. Once I was gone, life could return to normal. Watching those shadows from afar, I wished that I could change their heads—since I was just a kid, the word I thought was heads, not brains—but really, what if I had a way to change them?

Sure I was my mother's son from another relationship, but so what? It only caused me problems because they knew. If I could tinker with my abusive father's head, just a little, would he stop being so violent? And what if I could change a bunch of people at his company, to reach the underlying cause for his behavior? While I was at it, I could change my mom, and change my grandma, and myself. Imagine what it would be like if I could tinker with them, even just a little.

One of the four silhouettes disappeared, and my mom came outside through the front door. Though I was far away, she saw me standing in the middle of the street, carrying my leather satchel full of textbooks. But she was not at liberty to come down to where I was. Dad and Grandma were inside. My scrawny mom, who wet her hands and rubbed her frizzy hair to make it straight. Later, when I had pulled her from her family, a string of men whose names I can't remember had their way with her. I was unable to change my mother, just as I was unable to secure her affection. Perhaps in an attempt to over-come my failure to change her, I had become obsessed with my treatment of Yukari. As if I was refusing to cooperate with the structure of humanity, or with the facts of life.

What had I gained? Nothing.

Reaching this conclusion, I had to laugh. I had become preoccupied with the frustrations, contradictions and conflicts that make up a life. But now, I was in a place far removed from any of those things.

I did feel kind of sentimental for the days when I was still a member of the human race. Or at least aspired to be. The thought of that gave me a warm feeling for sure.

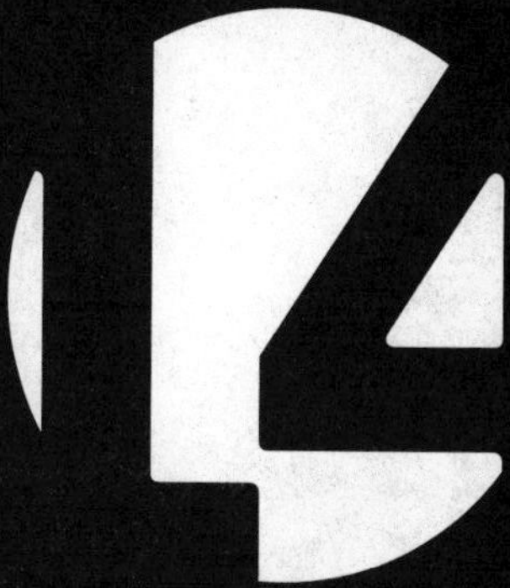

"... Give me the medicine."

"But I just did, remember?"

The doctor said the same thing as before.

"Then give me something else ... The trees outside,
no, the voices ..."

"... Voices?"

"I can hear Yukari ... screaming."

The doctor looked at me in silence. This seemed
like tacit encouragement.

"When I'm lying in bed, I hear Yukari screaming. The sound of her voice triggers a visual. Two guys filming her with a camcorder . . . and for some reason one of them is me."

The doctor's expression turned severe.

". . . You mean it's actually you?"

"No. It's not like that. More like it's all a movie that I know I've seen before, but not to the extent where I would actually believe that it was me in there. A lot like how it feels when I think about my sister or my mom. Or maybe with a bit more distance than that."

". . . That's your perversion talking."

"Also, my sister's legs. And broken bicycles . . ."

". . . What about her legs?"

"Nothing, forget it . . . by the way, what is that thing?"

I pointed at the wall. The white wall I could barely stand to look at.

"What the hell is that hook doing there? That metal hook. And why's there always a rope there? Strung in a knot?"

". . . Settle down now."

"How can I settle down? Give me medicine. Right now. The knot . . ."

"Knot?"

"I see Yukari in the knot. What is that thing!"

I snatched the doctor's lab coat. But the doctor didn't back away. He brought his face in close.

"You left it there."

I looked blankly at the doctor.

"Me?"

The doctor looked me in the eye.

"Who else would come in here and do that? I was shocked the first time that I saw it. But once, in the middle of the night, I watched you jump out of bed and loop the rope around the hook yourself . . . but when I came through the door . . . don't you remember? You laughed and said that you were only playing, then you fell asleep again. Practically passed out."

". . . No way."

"But I have to say, I think I understand the way you feel."

The doctor let go of me. His voice was gentle.

"Ours is a doctor-patient relationship. Understand? But if you'll permit me to speak my piece as a fellow human being . . . I'm amazed you're still alive."

". . . What?"

"It's amazing you're alive."

The aide who had been silent this whole time gave the doctor a worried look.

"Think back to all those years ago, when you pushed your sister off the cliff and injured her, then later on injured your mother. These things were a product of the evilness inside of you, though you couldn't have been fully conscious of it at the time . . . but you're conscious of it now, yes?"

"Yeah. For a while I had no clue who I was. So I clung on to any memories that I could get my hands on . . . after replaying those scenes in my head so many times, it's like I can feel everything happening, down to my sense of touch."

The doctor nodded.

"After that, you were sent off to the home for troubled youth, where you were rehabilitated. But you weren't actually fixed. Let me catch you up on what you haven't read. A doctor took you in, but you began to live each day with extreme caution. If somebody came close to you, the fear was difficult to bear, because you were afraid something inside of you might hurt them . . . but that was only an excuse. Quite simply, you hated being alive. Hated the world for bringing you into this. Nevertheless, you became a psychiatrist. In part so you could take over the family business from your taciturn new father, but you were also driven by a want to help people like you. Sorry to say, though, you weren't cut out for it. And then . . . you met her . . . Yukari."

He continued, expressionless.

"The rest should sound familiar. You were smitten. This was a love that shook you to the core. But as you've pointed out yourself, I suspect that it was only a projection of your mother. Which is to say, you used Yukari in an attempt to overwrite your past. As if retaliating against the world, by curing Yukari, could somehow save you in the process. Am I right? An attempt to convert these pesky black strings into something else."

"Maybe you're right. But I really did like Yukari . . . I don't understand it anymore."

"Exactly. You don't understand. It would have been all well and good if Yukari had been cured. Your love for Yukari was real, regardless of its underpinnings, and as a matter of fact, *there was one surefire way you could have saved Yukari*. But it's no use talking about that now . . . Why do you think Yukari hanged herself?"

"I mean . . ."

"It's all your fault."

Curiously, the aide placed a hand on the doctor's shoulder. But he continued.

"In all her other suicide attempts, she cut her wrists halfheartedly. In a sense, those times were all a cry for help. But in the end, she hanged herself. Just like her mother. In my opinion, this was the result of your obsessive focus on her treatment, which exerted a considerable influence on her brain. Your behavior was in fact so influential that the next time she attempted suicide, she gave up on cutting her wrists and stringed her neck instead. How about it? Sound plausible enough to you?"

I met eyes with the doctor. What he said made sense to me. Without me around, Yukari never would have died. She would still be alive, seeing Yoshimi for treatments. I nodded, but the doctor registered no reaction.

". . . Please try to remember. The day Yukari left you . . ."

". . . I can't . . . when my thoughts go there, something switches on inside of me . . . Give me some medicine. Please, I need it."

"You're going to imagine it for me. All the despair. And while you're at it, remember the day Yukari died."

"I can't."

"You failed to save the one person on earth who needed you the most . . . if I were you, I couldn't bear to live. I would have done the same thing as Yukari. You know, I'm much more sympathetic on the nights when you get up and loop that rope around the hook than I am right now."

"Meds."

". . . That's enough for today."

"Meds."

The doctor left and closed the door behind him. I felt short of breath. The room was suffocating. Claustrophobic. My eyes turned to the white wall. Not like I wanted to, but my eyes drifted over on their own. Yukari was hanging by the neck. Why was she looking at me like that? Oh, I get it. So you think I'd be better off if I stopped living too? I realized that the aide was standing in the room. His glasses were dirty.

". . . The doctor isn't giving me my medicine. You gotta help me."

"Yeah, I know. I have it right here."

I gobbled it down on the spot. But nothing happened.

"Is this real medicine?"

"Of course it is. What's wrong with you?"

Why was the man smiling? Or is that just the way he looked to me? I felt claustrophobic. Terrified. I couldn't take it. Then a voice. What voice? My sister screaming she had fallen off the cliff because of me? Yukari screaming at the camcorder?

"So . . . you've been tying knots."

"Yeah. Sounds like I have."

"Next time you make one, I'll come in and give you a boost."

". . . Huh?"

"Figured that would make things easier for you . . . I'll bet that an attempted suicide will get the doctor to give you a much stronger medicine. Right now he's only giving you enough to calm you down, in the best interest of your health. Worst case, you do actually die."

". . . What are you saying?"

"You can sleep beside Yukari's grave . . . the two of you can be together for eternity. I take it you've been watching Yukari hang herself?"

"Yeah. Most everyday. Wrapping the rope around her neck."

". . . You let her get away with that?"

The man stared at me. This was too much. The room was claustrophobic.

"If it was me, I'd stick my neck in there before she could and stop her."

I almost yelled at him. Actually, I guess I was already yelling. Next thing I knew, the man was gone. I banged on the door, rammed it with my shoulder, and banged away again. No medicine. I needed medicine. So claustrophobic. The trees were reaching at me through the windows. What was this voice? It was my voice. Is this what my voice sounded like? There was a darkness in the room. Underneath the bed. Something there. Something was definitely there. Please stop. My mom was underneath the bed, sleeping with some random guy. Is that why I couldn't sleep? Yukari, Yukari in the photo . . .

[Unprinted File]

While I was in the examination room, Wakui came in to check on me. He didn't say a word.

The burden on my consciousness had transformed into an attack on Mamiya. Wakui was concerned that if I kept this up I might go crazy, too. Though that was hardly a concern. For a while he had said that we should get it over with and kill them both, but lately he had given up on saying so.

". . . Almost there, huh," Wakui said quietly. His voice a little tired.

"Yeah. I'd say we've been about half successful . . . if we had done as well as the old Soviet or American armies, we would have really rounded out our revenge. I could have implanted myself into his head completely. I mean, if he was totally brainwashed, he would have brought himself to ruin, convinced my troubles were his own."

"Compared to Kida, though, I'd say things with Mamiya are going well. Might even call this good enough. Not like I know what I'm talking about . . . By the way, he's passed out."

"Good. Go set up the knot."

"Already did."

". . . I'd like to leave him to his own devices for a while."

I realized there was music playing in the room.

From the way Wakui looked at me, I must

have done something that surprised him. Wonder what. Maybe it was that I turned the music off before the chorus.

Outside it was raining. The rain that was irrelevant to us.

"You really know how to communicate with people . . . without hurting their feelings." I looked at Wakui as I told him so. "You're so careful about what people think . . . but it's pretty common . . . the sort of thing that people carry over from childhood. Like if you're always playing the peacekeeper for your parents . . . sorry . . . I guess this might not come across as complimentary."

Wakui cracked a smile, making his skinny eyes look even skinnier.

"Not at all. Like you said, I've gotten this far keeping something of a distance from the world . . . so if I really am as careful as you say, maybe it's a sort of barrier for me."

I looked again at Wakui, seated in the corner of the room, by the window, legs crossed. He was getting pretty thin. When I realized how long his nails had grown, I looked away and spoke again.

"There's a lot that we don't know about each other . . . but maybe this distance is a good thing . . . When I'm with you, I don't feel the tension that I always feel with other people. If someone saw us from afar, we'd look like a pretty odd couple."

This made Wakui smile.

"I wish we could have met up at a bar somewhere . . . but I dunno," Wakui said. I started wondering again about the music that was playing a few minutes before. "This goes beyond Yukari. You and I have lost something essential to our lives. You especially . . . so if things start going poorly, and we need to kill them with our own two hands, I want for you to let me do it."

Look at him, button-up shirt made with quality fabric, well-groomed hair. Though lately, it felt like Wakui was trying a bit too hard to keep up appearances. As if keeping himself looking tidy kept him human. Sometimes he walked around with dirty glasses. He used to wear a wristwatch from A. Lange & Söhne, but lately he forgot to put it on.

"So do you—" I started saying, but I was unable to finish.

Wakui turned to face me, but eventually cast his gaze out the window. On the irrelevant rain and the irrelevant landscape.

After Wakui had left the room, I lit a cigarette. My thoughts turned to a reoccurring dream I used to have.

There is a huge crowd of people, heading in every direction. I'm trying to get somewhere, but I'm stopped at what appears to be a baggage checkpoint at an airport. The guy who works there, I guess the security guard, he sees my bag and cries out frantically, "What the hell is this?" and takes my bag away. "What the hell is this? Come on, not this too." He won't let up. "Look at this stuff," he says. "You serious?"

Then he asks me.

"Just what do you think you're doing with this stuff?" People who were way behind me in the line are passing by me now. "Can you explain to me why you would need these things?"

As you may imagine, I am unable to respond.

I wondered why I didn't have this dream anymore.

15

When I awoke in darkness, the knot was floating in midair.

The room was claustrophobic. But maybe the knot was a way out. What was this? I was flying high. Like I could pull off anything I tried.

Step. I needed something to step up on. There was a chair just the right size. What a perfect chair for the task. Why not try it out? Yeah, try it on for size. Try out the knot.

My pulse quickened. Head full of blood. I felt afraid.
Yukari appeared before me. Face tormented with pain,
she draped the knot around her neck. My sister, tumbling down the cliff. When Yukari died, the strength
emptied from my legs. The scene was planted in my
brain like a brutal cinematic sequence. Can't have that.
I couldn't bear to go through that again.

Can't have that, I told myself. The knot was up for
grabs. I shot my neck in first. Unlike the last time, I
was able to stand up. Staggering like when Yukari died,
but nevertheless upright. Able to extricate Yukari from
the knot.

Strength marshalled in my body, as if to counteract
the leaden feeling in my head. A warmth spread through
me. What could stop me now? Such were my thoughts.
Saving Yukari would be hit or miss. *Save Yukari, hit or
miss*. I stepped onto the chair and took the knot in
hand. What were my odds? The odds of saving Yukari?
And the odds of failing? What did it matter? Slipping
a knot around my neck. How could that save Yukari?

My pulse ran wild. Different in kind from how it felt
before. Where was I now? Out with a group of friends,
climbing a wooded slope, collecting bugs. We found

a girl caught in a heap of tires and wrecked bicycles, against a backdrop of dark trees. Was this . . . my sister? But if I was on top of the hill, how could I be seeing her from below? It felt as if the trees were closing in.

My heart beat even faster. What was going on? Discovering the injured girl, I thought she was so beautiful. If only she was older. Like my teacher. Sometimes she wore short skirts. If only she was banged up with her clothes torn, like the girl. Her clothes were torn, her pretty pale legs bared. Seeing them made me aroused. I mean it made me hard. For the first time ever. The trees around me swayed, as if to egg me on. Closing around the girl, they swayed in waves that grew and grew . . . I felt something approaching. Had I hurt Yukari? Had my experience finding the girl made the idea of trashing women morbidly exciting . . . ? If I could be content with that, I was a monster, but at that young age, could I be blamed for my arousal, when I saw the girl?

Something was coming. A memory of skiing. White snow . . . My head hurt. Something was in the way. My sister tumbling down the cliff, my mom surrounded by the men. I was imbued with the despair of losing

Yukari. Feeling rocked, I reached to grab ahold of something. My neck was in the knot. I shot my fingers through. Between my neck and the rope. I had to lift my body up. Otherwise I'd break my neck. Something was expanding in my head. Topping up.

Did something happen? Had I stepped off the chair? Had memories of my sister and my mom stopped something from returning? Was that what moved my feet? But why? What was I resisting? Me? My strength was gone. Call the doctor. But I had no voice. Not enough strength. Fingers pinched against my neck. I couldn't breathe. Had to find a place to step. My feet. But what? My feet, but then my body swayed. Swaying made it worse. Something to step on. It hurts—a step—before my eyes—is that—a woman?

WAKUI TOOK A sip of coffee and admired the painting on the wall. An abstract painting of intersecting lines, forming geometric patterns. Kozuka was drinking coffee too.

"... That finishes that."

"Yeah."

Wakui looked up, as if about to speak, but paused, then almost spoke again. Kozuka beat him to it, staring down into his coffee cup.

". . . We can dispose of Mamiya's corpse any number of ways. One option is to report it as a patient suicide. Or we could simply bury him . . . he had been crashing with friends anyway and had no permanent address. His existence was already so precarious, and now he's disappeared. If the police find the body, they'll start making moves, but otherwise they'll probably let well alone."

Wakui nodded. He thought the doctor had been looking awfully thin the past few days. It was well established that their revenge was a collaboration, only he couldn't help but think the burden on Kozuka had been far too heavy. Wakui attempted to lighten his load, but it was no use. He had barely even qualified as an assistant. He knew where he was coming from. He recognized that taking matters into your own hands went above and beyond assuming responsibility. It was a way of setting up a barrier against the world.

The least he could do was dispose of Mamiya's corpse. However shared the terms of the revenge had been in theory, his actual contribution had been scarce. Wakui was about to say as much, but Kozuka continued.

"Mamiya lived a pitiful life. Loitering downtown until somebody picked him up, which happened regularly on account of his good looks . . . but those women were playing with fire. His violence wasted them away. Soon enough, they recognized him as a hazard to their lives. He was a piece of trash they never should have picked up off the ground."

Kozuka curiously eyed his empty coffee cup. Maybe he had been unable to taste its flavor. To a café owner like Wakui, the shock of someone losing the ability to taste coffee was especially shocking. Bearing this in mind, Wakui tried making Kozuka's coffee extra strong, but so far he had failed to notice any change in his reaction.

It's quiet, thought Wakui, feeling an inexplicable sadness. Turns out after a person dies it's really quiet, huh. The hospital was much too far from town. Glancing outside, he realized that the foliage was beginning to change color, but this failed to inspire any change in his emotions. Wakui looked at Kozuka and spoke.

". . . Let me ask you something."

"Go ahead," said Kozuka.

Wakui took a short breath, preparing to respond. This had been on his mind for quite some time.

"I read your notes. I mean, you told me it was okay if I read them, so I did. I can't speak to what you're writing now, on the computer . . . but in what I've read so far, there's a part where you and Yukari make love with each other . . . you and Yukari, in the examination room . . . What made you include that scene?"

"Because it helped me solve a riddle."

Kozuka held up a piece of paper. The article about the slasher, printed out.

An unemployed man in his twenties stabbed a number of people on the street.

". . . What is this?"

YOSHIMI WELCOMED KOZUKA like a patient as usual.

"Mamiya is dead."

Kozuka set the suitcase on the carpet and sat facing Yoshimi at the round table.

". . . Where you going?" Yoshimi asked.

"Out of the country."

"Running away?"

"No, I'm coming back eventually."

Yoshimi poured some wine for Kozuka. Every other time he had declined, but now he took a sip.

"So I guess this is the last time I'll be seeing you."

The air conditioning was on too high. Yoshimi never noticed, but today neither did Kozuka.

"Viewing this world from a distance," said Yoshimi, "all the different lines extend into a network. The lines exert their influence beyond our personal perception, sometimes pushing us to act, against our will. Like with you and Yukari. How you projected your feelings for your mother. Our lives are so much smaller than the lives that we imagine for ourselves."

"Yeah . . . and you were a part of that network too."

". . . Hm?"

"Because you were the one who told Mamiya where to find Yukari."

A train passed in the distance. The people on board fraught with their preoccupations, each of them being carried off somewhere. Yoshimi stared blankly at Kozuka.

"The story goes that Kida just so happened to dis-cover Yukari working at Wakui's café. Not impossible. But I get the sense you tipped him off."

"Hard to say. No proof."

—*Those guys who called Yukari out at the café. It's going to feel great.*

"What was that?" Yoshimi asked.

Kozuka held up a digital recorder.

"Your voice. I recorded our last session together. How did you know Yukari had been working at the café? And how did you know the café was where those guys approached Yukari? At first this went over my head, but after everything, when I listened to it all from the beginning, I finally realized something was out of place. I guess you could say it opened up my field of vision. Kida found Yukari at the café on his own, but since you were the one who tipped them off, you assumed they went together. And before I even started coming by here, you seemed to know all about my likes and tastes. You were keeping tabs on all of us. And another thing. You told a lie."

"About?"

"You said you fixed my head when we were at the

home for troubled youth. But you didn't really fix me, did you?"

A pillar light in one corner of the room began to flicker.

"The slasher case involving one of your patients happened before I ever met you. At which point you were already screwed up . . . I wrote those notes. Wrote my life story, so I could force Kida and Mamiya to read it. But I think my reasons went beyond that. I was of a mind to write my story down. But I told a lie myself . . . Wonder why. Maybe I was being aspirational. While I was writing, I veered away from the facts. After leaving the treatment center, I was chased by this lingering impression that I had slept with my own mom. When I tore apart the kitchen and she got cut by a broken plate. I had this vision of knocking her down and sleeping with her, then and there. This never happened. I was absolutely sure. And yet I couldn't help but feel like I had done it anyway. My actual memory of it not happening felt somehow out of place to me . . . I talked to a doctor about it. Not you, obviously. He told me it was not uncommon to imagine assaulting your mother, so not to worry. Probably just buried guilt coming to the surface. But the impression was so graphic. You hypnotized me into thinking that it happened. Over the course of my treatment. Isn't that right? Walking an impressionable kid like me through all the textures of the female body. In great detail."

". . . No proof."

"Sure. But an inescapable conclusion after everything I've heard from you." Kozuka spoke without changing his expression. "It was bad enough I had been raised in a sexually problematic environment. But working with you at the treatment center totally screwed up my perception of sex. I can't have sex with women. That's why I never slept with Yukari.

"She was sure I thought she was dirty. Our first try was a failure, so we gave it time, but after the fourth or fifth attempt, Yukari started crying. After that, she stopped letting me try. Spending time with me was hurting her . . . Being rejected by me made her want to kill herself again. I tried explaining how I felt to her. But she didn't believe me. Watching her lose her memory and leave me for Wakui was extremely painful, but it was a blessing for Yukari . . .

"So why'd you do a thing like that to such a little

kid? Forget it. I can answer for you. You were screwing with me. Weren't you? Now I understand what made you send Yukari to my clinic . . . You thought it would be funny if I lost the ability to have sex with women. Not like it was a conscious thought. But it was there all right, in the back of your mind. Same as you thought it would be funny if Yukari and I fell into the peculiar sort of romance that can only happen between a psychiatrist and patient. Funny, right? You get a kick out of meddling with human behavior. And I did almost exactly what you had in mind. I understand now that I've entered your domain. Just an evil old man, killing time. Once age had made you give up all your other interests, you were left with nothing but the perverse nature you had fostered all these years. Maybe it was all a twisted act of love toward Yukari. The only reason that you told your colleague to adopt me was to give yourself a front row seat for your pet project."

Kozuka stared Yoshimi down.

"I want my life back."

Yoshimi had nothing to say. Just sat there, lazing in his chair.

". . . I have something to show you." Kozuka opened

up the suitcase and smirked. "I'm not leaving the country. There's nothing in here yet. This suitcase is for you. You never would have fit when you were big and strong, but now you'll pop right in."

The men met eyes. The pillar in the corner went on flickering. Yoshimi must have thought that he would look away, but Kozuka's gaze was rigid. Yoshimi smiled through a sigh.

"All right . . . Settle down. Care for some water?"

Yoshimi lifted his hips from his chair, but Kozuka gestured for him to stop.

"No chance," he said. "I know what you're about to do . . . You're getting up to push the help button by the refrigerator. Too bad you'll never make it. The second you stand up, I'll knock you down. Honestly, the thought of you pounding on that button is too much. Are you really so fond of life? You call this living?"

". . . How are you going to fit me in there?"

"The idea was to make you fall asleep, but I forgot the drugs . . . so I'm going to beat you within an inch of your life."

". . . An old man like me? But you . . . No, you have it in you. State you're in."

The air conditioning was humming. Keeping the room cool, despite the time of year. Kozuka lit a cigarette, not bothering to ask if he could smoke in the apartment. Smoke drifted from his face.

"If you try to bite your tongue off, I'll rip your dentures out. That way you won't be able to bite through."

". . . Makes sense."

Kozuka made Yoshimi stand. He showed no sign of resisting.

"For the record, you've never done it once?"

"Not really . . . Except for one time, when I went to a sex shop and we made it work after a struggle. The woman was real nice. Such a nice woman . . . But just once. That was the only time it ever worked. Maybe I can't do it with a person that I love . . . As you can see, your strange little project was almost totally successful. But now your monster of a patient is going to take his turn."

Yoshimi fit into the suitcase. Before snapping it shut, Kozuka peered inside. Yoshimi took the opportunity to speak.

"I was wondering what made you research Tsutomu Miyazaki and Hiroshi Maeue . . . but it makes perfect sense. They were both sexually deranged."

". . . Only one thing matters now: the black strings running from me to you. Aren't they beautiful?"

WHEN THEY OPENED the suitcase, Yoshimi winced at the brightness of the lights. To someone on the verge of death, even the faithfulness with which the body transmits pain becomes a little dear. Yoshimi stood up, nearly tipping himself over. There was another man with them in the room. A skittish looking guy, stuck to his chair and looking at Kozuka and Yoshimi like he was terrified.

"This is Kida . . . Hey, that's odd."

Kozuka gave Kida a look of confusion.

"When you see the old man, you're supposed to kill him and then kill yourself. Why do you think I hypnotized you? . . . Looks like it isn't working out."

Kida twitched with terror. Kozuka sighed.

"Maybe the medicine is still affecting him. Things went better with Mamiya than they did with this one here, but I did manage to insert myself into his mind . . . Anyway, he'll murder you eventually . . . Until he does, you'll be spending every single day together.

Don't worry, we'll feed you. And we'll put something on your chart, just for fun. Later on, you can tell me the most interesting ailment you encountered as a doctor."

Kozuka headed for the door.

"I'll have you know, Yoshimi. Yukari did manage to break free from the net you always talk about, however briefly. Granted only after I erased her memory, a method usually deemed unforgivable, and making life considerably harder for myself . . . but then you came along, like some referee of evildoing, and dropped her back into the net . . . Rest assured, your death will not be left to cancer or senility."

Kozuka opened the door.

"What does it mean for a person to be alive?"

He closed the door behind him. This far from town, the world outside was silent.

In the confines of the room, Yoshimi turned to face the other man. He would make an effort to diagnose his condition, drawing from his long career in psychiatric medicine. Taking a short breath, he looked him over for a moment, but told himself it was a waste of time. This man had irreparably lost his mind, to an extent that he had never seen in decades working as a doctor.

What a hack, thought Yoshimi. This likely meant his own death would be all too sloppy.

KOZUKA AND WAKUI sat across from each other, drinking coffee.

"Shame I didn't get to see it," said Wakui. Though he didn't look as if he really thought it was a shame.

"Sorry about that. It happened so quick. All I saw through the window of the door were the last moments of his life."

Kozuka adjusted his posture. The folding chair below him creaked, the dry sound of metal against metal.

". . . I suspect, however, that Kida strangling Yoshimi had nothing to do with my hypnosis or my memories. When the drugs wore off, he went ballistic and Yoshimi's neck took the brunt of it . . . Yoshimi went limp, not even resisting."

"What about Kida?"

"Hanged himself about four days later. Doubt that had anything to do with me either. He got worked up and went too far, that's all. Too bad that things turned

out that way. But I dunno, I guess it wasn't all that bad
. . . If I were a genius, maybe I could have used the
memories I gave them to induce dissociative identity
disorder, or you know, multiple personality disorder, to
make those memories override their personalities. So
that my very self took root inside of them, as memory
personified . . . I feel like we came really close."

Wakui nodded. Like he was plenty satisfied. Kozuka
said more.

"I buried the corpse. No one's the wiser. As ritzy as
Yoshimi's building was, they had no cameras out back
to watch me leaving with the suitcase. They do have
one out front, but when a group of yakuza moved in,
they badgered the management until they removed the
one from the back door . . . As long as they have no
lead on the body, he'll be just another old man reported
missing."

". . . Listen, Kozuka."

Turning slowly toward him, Wakui gave Kozuka a
steady look. Kozuka was still working on his coffee. It
did not appear that he could taste it.

"After Yukari died, I lost the strength to live." Wakui's
voice was trembling. "I thought as long as those guys

died, as long as we made sure of it and finished taking our revenge, I would be able to let go of being alive . . . As you've already guessed, before meeting Yukari, I had my own ups and downs. Running that hip café felt like some kind of a joke. Meeting her gave me a reason to give life another chance . . . I wasn't really so attached to life at all."

Kozuka listened, drinking his coffee like it was a cup of warm water.

"But now . . . I'm eager for another go at life. I'm even thinking about setting up shop again. Know what, though, Kozuka?" Wakui said, looking his way. "I bet you had something to do with this."

Kozuka emptied his cup of coffee and looked at Wakui. He was grinning.

"Psychiatrists can't work miracles," he told Wakui. "You came to that conclusion on your own."

"Nah, I'm certain you had something to do with this."

". . . I would be in trouble without you alive. If you had died, there would be no one left who knew about Yukari . . . Please hold on to all your memories of her for me."

"What about you?" Tears were forming in Wakui's eyes.

"Forget about me. Just let me ask you this."

"Sure."

"When you gave Yukari . . . sexual attention, surrounding her with love and affection, in a way I never could . . . did she look happy?"

"Yes."

Wakui started crying.

"Is that right." Kozuka's voice was trembling. "I'm glad to hear it . . . really glad."

ALONE NOW, KOZUKA opened the door of the room. The doll of Yukari was gone. His notes had been destroyed, the memory of the computer blank.

Kozuka had not given Wakui the whole story about how things ended for Yoshimi.

In fact, he had seen Yoshimi being strangled by Kida through the window in the door. But then Yoshimi saw that Kozuka was outside. His voice was inaudible through the door, but his lips were moving. As if, while being strangled, he was offering a causal hello to an acquaintance who he hadn't seen in a little while. Because he was bent over backward, his face was upside down for Kozuka. There seemed to be no trace of suffering. Like he was saying: "Hey, you made it. Good luck living an honest life."

That face came back to Kozuka, making him feel dizzy enough he vomited. Down on all fours, he was struggling to breathe, and fumbled for the handle of the drawer. He dumped whatever medicine he found into his mouth. How many pills was that? Ever since discovering Mamiya's hanging corpse, he had been secretly craving medicine. Or maybe the cauterizing effects of his last session with Yoshimi were beginning to wear off. It took some time for him to manage to stand up.

His head was heavy. At this rate, it felt like it was over, he was dying. The conclusion of his life. But he could not let that happen. It would mean that he had been defeated by the world. Which is why he was standing at the ECT terminal. Slightly modified, so that he could operate it by himself.

This is the sort of life I wish I could have lived, he thought. A modest enough ambition. To be alone someplace, no company, able to spend my time taking walks and reading books. He wanted to become a different person. Not saddled with a mind like this one, but a little simpler. On the table was a single sheet of paper, listing the PINs for his debit and credit cards and the address of a small apartment he had newly leased. He had even hired a lawyer to offload the hospital.

Once the ECT was finished, and he was empty, he would discover the other stack of pages. Another life, which he had written for himself, alongside the story in the manuscript. It was a fanciful sham of a life, from its ordinary beginnings up through the ordinary present.

Born into a family of four, he met his first girlfriend in high school, and dated somebody in college who he thought that he might marry, but they broke up. He had seen several women after that, but now he was alone. In his spare time he liked to travel, and was surprisingly fond of funny TV shows, and also enjoyed books and music. His every idea was ordinary. Hopefully he would be able to believe all this about himself.

One spot had given him some trouble, but here is how he finally described it: You used to date a woman named Yukari, but you parted ways. Now she is running a café in Los Angeles with a really decent guy. She has a quiet, happy life. Obviously these words were meaningless. But he was unable to stop himself from writing them. As if they were a prayer made in the face of an unflappable reality.

This may be my last cigarette, he told himself, and sparked his lighter. When I open my eyes, maybe I won't remember that I was a smoker. Watching the smoke, he wondered what would happen if things didn't go as planned. What if he still remembered everything, even after going through the gauntlet of intense ECT. Or what if he forgot, but temporarily, only to remember later? The chances of that were exceedingly high.

He told himself it was a gamble. A question of whether or not he would let it happen. If the gamble was a failure, and he was returned to his former self, he would continue to live life as a psychiatrist. To do his best to mitigate the damage of the countless black strings swarming in the background of the world. By ending the lives of those two guys, he had seriously impaired his own mind. Payback for breaching the limits of his psyche. No more would he expect to derive happiness from life. Like a piece of machinery, or a person whose real life has ended, he would continue living merely in the service of his patients.

Though he truly wished he could experience a different life. However briefly. To sample some of the tranquility of the world, which had so thoroughly evaded him.

Kozuka rubbed out his cigarette and reached for the switch of the ECT machine. The telephone rang. Must be Wakui, he thought.

There was something that Kozuka had never been able to tell Wakui. He was the spitting image of that actor, the one that Kozuka told Yukari her old boyfriend looked like, when he was feeding her those stories under hypnosis.

Through the tears, Kozuka muttered an apology to Wakui. The phone rang off the hook. He flicked the switch.

AFTERWORD TO THE PAPERBACK EDITION

This novel is the paperback edition of my seventeenth book.

Questions about what it means to be human, and what it means to exist in the world, are central to me—as they are for many authors—and in this book, I wound up exploring these questions at length.

Looking back, I suppose one reason why these questions are so central to me is that when I was little, I was unable to honestly accept (in other words, get used to) the world for what it is.

This story was born in the wake of *Cult X* and *The Night You Disappeared*. Personally, I suspect the structure of the book owes much to my experience with another of my novels, *Last Winter, We Parted*. I also think the atmosphere of my earlier work shows up here in places like the "stack of pages."

While the same applies to all my novels, this book turned out to be a special thing to me. The final passage with the telephone, as some of you might have noticed, is something of a tie-in with another of my novels.

If this book, whether in its overall shape or in its details, has brought about some kind of feeling in my readers, then I consider my work, as its creator, a success.

27 May 2019

Fuminori Nakamura

(Author's Note: While it is often said that the results of experiments with subliminal messaging were fraudulent, it is also said that a different set of similar experiments clearly demonstrated its effectiveness. For the sections on Tsutomu Miyazaki, I mainly used reference materials to access the facts of the case, but the analysis of his character is my own. There really was a person like "Taka" in his life, but following the practice of my resources, I opted for a pseudonym.)

SELECTED BIBLIOGRAPHY

夢のなか―連続幼女殺害事件被告の告白 [In a Dream: Confessions of an Accused Serial Killer of Little Girls]. Tsutomu Miyazaki. Tsukuru Shuppan. ISBN: 4924718300.

夢のなか、いまも―連続幼女殺害事件元被告の告白 [Still in a Dream: Confessions of an Accused Serial Killer of Little Girls, After the Trial]. Tsutomu Miyazaki. Tsukuru Shuppan. ISBN: 4924718726.

宮崎勤裁判 [The Trial of Tsutomu Miyazaki]. Three volumes. Ryuzo Saki. Asahi Press. ISBN: 402256329X (vol. 1), 4022571985 (vol. 2), 4022571993 (vol. 3).

宮崎勤　精神鑑定書―「多重人格説」を検証する [Tsutomu Miyazaki: Expert Psychological Opinion— Inquiry into the "Split Personality" Theory].

Takino Takahiro. Kodansha. ISBN:
4062085437.

宮崎勤事件―塗り潰されたシナリオ [The Tsutomu
Miyazaki Case: The Painted-Over Script].
Fumiya Ichihashi. Shincho Bunko. ISBN:
4101426244.

M／世界の、憂鬱な先端 [M: The Despondent Fringes of
the World]. Shinobu Yoshioka. Bungei Bunko.
ISBN: 4167547031.

マインド・コントロール [Mind Control]. Takashi Okada.
Bungeishunju. ISBN: 4166610740.

記憶のしくみ [Memory: From Mind to Molecules]. Two
volumes. Larry R. Squire and Eric R. Kandel.
Kodansha. ISBN: 4062578425 (vol. 1),
4062578433 (vol. 2).